Other books by
Colleen O'Shaughnessy McKenna

Too Many Murphys
Fourth Grade Is a Jinx
Fifth Grade: Here Comes Trouble
Eenie, Meanie, Murphy, No!
Murphy's Island
Merry Christmas, Miss McConnell!
The Truth About Sixth Grade

Mother Murphy

Colleen O'Shaughnessy McKenna

**SCHOLASTIC
HARDCOVER**

Scholastic Inc.
New York

Library of Congress Cataloging-in-Publication Data

McKenna, Colleen O'Shaughnessy.
  Mother Murphy / Colleen O'Shaughnessy McKenna.
    p.   cm.
  Summary: When Mrs. Murphy has to get off her feet because she's
expecting a baby, Collette takes over with surprising results.

ISBN 0-590-44820-X

  [1. Mothers — Fiction.   2. Babies — Fiction.   3. Family life —Fiction.]
I. Title.
PZ7.M478675Mo   1992
[Fic] — dc20   90-23315
                                                                    CIP
                                                                     AC

12 11 10 9 8 7 6 5 4 3 2 1   2 3 4 5 6 7/9

Printed in the U.S.A.   37

First Scholastic printing, March 1992

*This book is dedicated to all of the people at Scholastic Inc.
who lovingly nurture me through each and every book.*

Chapter One

"Anybody for hot chocolate?" Collette carefully set the tray and clattering mugs down on her dresser top. "I made it myself, so pretend it's great."

"Thanks. Wow, just look at all that snow!" laughed Marsha. "If this keeps up, we will have perfect skiing weather on Saturday."

Collette looked over at Sarah and smiled. "Great!" Sarah just rolled her eyes and shivered. She had never been skiing and was still a little nervous about the Seven Springs ski trip. Marsha was thrilled to be able to show off her Bloomingdale's hot-pink ski outfit with matching goggles, and Collette was just plain worried that she wouldn't be able to go at all. It was already Monday and her parents were *still* thinking about it.

"Seven Springs is over two hours away, Collette," her mother had pointed out last night. "Skiing is such a fast sport. If anything happened to you, they would have to send an ambulance down to Children's Hospital!"

"Mom!" Collette had cried. "I'm going skiing, not into the jungle to hunt tigers."

Collette's father had laughed, but when he finally folded his paper and looked at Collette, he didn't seem too happy with the idea either. "Collette, you've only been skiing three times. Why don't you let me take you and the little guys up next Sunday and I'll give you a few pointers? I really agree with your mother. You're not old enough to go off on your own."

Collette flopped back against the pillows, looking up at the bottom slats of her little sister's top bunk. When would she be old enough? Her parents wouldn't let her go off on her own until she was walking down the aisle to get married. And even then her dad would be right by her side. The ski trip sounded like a lot of fun! Sarah and Marsha were both eleven and *their* parents signed each permission slip as soon as it hit the kitchen table. Why did Collette's parents have to make such a big deal out of everything? Collette wasn't allowed to do anything fun until she was older and it was *impossible* to get older in her house.

She still shared a room with a seven year old and her two younger brothers were always bursting into her room to toss their dirty socks at her friends or make burping noises to shock them. Her dad was nice to offer to take her skiing on Sunday, but she would rather stay home than march into the lodge at Seven Springs with her dad, a nine-year-old brother, a little sister who would ask Collette to get her in and out of her boots every ten minutes, and wild person Stevie. Even though Stevie was finally five years old, he still acted more like a large dog than a kid. He would whoop around the lodge, making everyone turn around, and then go off the highest, most dangerous slope at Seven Springs, screaming, "Hey, Collette, watch my trick!" as he bolted away.

"Collette! Collette Murphy!"

Collette sat up and turned. Marsha lay on the bed beside her and swatted her with a stuffed rabbit. "You were in never-never land, lady. Now when are you going to know for positive sure if you can go on Saturday?"

"Please go, Collette." Sarah clasped her hands in prayer. "I need you there for moral support. I just know I'll fall off the ski lift. I wish they had elevators!"

Collette and Marsha laughed. Sarah had moved from Fort Lauderdale to Pittsburgh in the second grade, and she had been making excuses ever since for not going skiing or ice-skating.

"I like my feet to stay flat on the ground," she'd insist. But this year even Sarah was excited about Saturday. Sixth- and seventh-graders from three Catholic schools would be there. P.T.A. groups had lots of food planned, and a live band would play until nine. It was practically a prom!

"Everyone is going, Collette," Marsha said. She pulled a piece of paper from her back pocket and grabbed a pen from Collette's dresser. "Okay, the 'for-sures' from the sixth grade are: me, of course; Sarah, who is not allowed to chicken out; Roger, who I hope and pray *does* chicken out; David, Michael, Jamie, Megan . . ." Marsha stopped and

4

looked up at Collette. "So, do I add your name while there is still room on my paper?"

"My mom said you could *both* spend the night since the bus gets in so late," Sarah said. "We could come home and make hot chocolate . . ."

Marsha nudged Collette. "And talk about all those cute seventh-grade boys who followed us around begging to carry our skis."

Collette laughed. "The seventh-graders ignore us in school, Marsha. They will ignore us even more at the ski lodge. We will have Roger and his band of loonies chasing us with snowballs."

Marsha hopped off the bed and pulled Collette to her feet. "Come on, Collette. Time to go downstairs and ask your mom for her final verdict."

Sarah grabbed her other arm. "Yeah, I bet when your mom sees your two best friends at your side, both of us promising to protect you, she will let you go."

"She will *insist* that you go!" Marsha laughed.

Collette allowed herself to be led down the staircase. On the landing, Stevie whizzed past them, a worried look on his face. "Collette, go downstairs fast!"

"What's wrong, Stevie? Did you break something?" Stevie usually ran up and hid in his closet when he was in trouble.

"No — I have to get a washcloth for Mommy's head. She's throwing up a whole bunch."

Collette took the rest of the steps in two leaps. She ran down the hall and knocked on the bathroom door.

"Mom, are you all right?"

She didn't hear anything for a few seconds, then the toilet flushed and water ran in the sink.

Finally her mother opened the door. She wiped under each eye with a tissue and then ran her fingers through her long dark hair. "I'm fine, honey. I just felt — "

Collette's eyes grew huge as her mother covered her mouth again and slammed the door. Even though the toilet kept flushing, Collette could hear her mother getting sick again and again.

"What's wrong?" whispered Marsha. Sarah stood in the hall, biting her thumbnail.

"She's fine," said Collette quickly, her ear glued to the door. But she was worried. Mothers usually never got sick, especially when friends were over.

Stevie came running downstairs, holding two

dripping washcloths and an armload of towels. "We can wrap her up in all these towels. Is she okay? Make Daddy come home!"

Again Collette said that her mother was fine. But this time she said it more softly, and believed it less.

Marsha pulled Stevie away from the door. "Hey, Steve, do you want to come over to my house and see my new Nintendo game? It's so hard I can't get off the first board! I need your help."

Stevie grinned and dropped the towels. "Okay!" Then he frowned and bent to pick them up. "I have to stay here and take care of Mommy," he said seriously. "I don't think she's ever throwed up before."

"Collette," Marsha whispered. "We have to go now but call me as soon as you ask your mom about Saturday. Do you know when that might be?"

Collette nodded. But when the bathroom door finally opened and Collette saw her mother's red watery eyes, she knew it wasn't now.

Chapter Two

"Are you sure you're okay, Mom?" Collette held the cup of steaming tea out to her mother. "When did you get the flu?"

Her mother just smiled. "I don't think it's the flu. I feel fine now. In fact, I feel a little silly lying down when it's almost time to start dinner."

"Collette is going to cook it," announced Laura. "She already got out a box of macaroni and a jar of applesauce, and a jar of . . . what else, Collette?"

"Peanut butter, in case the macaroni doesn't turn out too hot." Collette was glad to see her mother smile.

"That sounds great. Stevie, you and Jeff go down and help set the table, okay? And Laura, would you go downstairs in the laundry room and carry up the big pile of folded towels?"

Everyone was trying their hardest to help. As soon as Stevie had run through the house shouting that their mom was throwing up, no one wanted to watch cartoons, play Nintendo, or do anything but make sure she was better. Moms were kind of like teachers, some of them went years without missing a day on the job.

As soon as everyone else left the room, Mrs. Murphy sat up in bed and took the ice pack from her head. "Don't tell Laura I took this off, honey, but my forehead needs defrosting."

Collette laughed. "Wait till you see the peanut-butter sandwich Jeff made you. It's about three inches thick, and he added lettuce. Jeff says that it's full of protein to fight off your germs."

Mrs. Murphy smiled, then grew serious and took Collette's hand. "I don't think I have any germs, Collette."

Collette nodded, hoping her mother wasn't offended or anything. "Most people have germs, especially if they're throwing up."

"Collette, thanks for taking such good care of me. I feel much better. What would I do without you, sweetie? You have always been such a help to me. You know, I still remember the day I found out I was pregnant with you." Mrs. Murphy smiled and leaned over to push back Collette's blonde hair. "I was so excited that I hugged the nurse who gave me the results. And now here you are playing nurse to me. Time goes by so quickly."

Collette grinned. No matter how many times she heard stories about the "good old days," they still sounded great.

A sudden gust of wind rattled outside the windows. Collette and her mother looked at each other and raised their eyebrows. A snowstorm warning had been announced all afternoon.

"We don't need any more snow," groaned Mrs. Murphy, shivering and pulling up the quilt. "Want to snuggle for a minute?"

Collette leaned back next to her mother and pulled up the other end of the quilt. In a minute she would have to go downstairs and help Jeff and Stevie find the right silverware, and then try to make macaroni that didn't stick together in one five-pound ball that no one wanted to eat. But for right now, curling up next to her mom felt great, just like old times.

"As soon as Daddy gets home, I want the snow to fall for hours and hours," said Collette. "It's like being inside a paperweight. Besides, then the skiing will be absolutely perfect on Saturday. Mom . . ." Collette leaned up on one elbow and smiled. "I heard that a mom from St. Paul's is carving a penguin out of ice for a centerpiece for the party at Seven Springs. There's going to be lots of cheese, bologna, pepperoni, and piles and piles of hot wings. Someone's dad is donating twenty pounds of potato salad."

Her mother looked impressed and then closed her eyes. "Collette, please . . . I'm sorry, honey, but don't mention food right now. . . ." Mrs. Murphy sat up and pressed the ice bag to her forehead. "In fact, maybe you'd better move the trash can next to the bed."

"Mom!" Collette scrambled out of bed and knelt down in front of her mother. "Should I call Daddy? Does he have any idea that you're *this* sick?"

Mrs. Murphy nodded, then smiled. "Yes, honey. Daddy *knows* all about how dizzy and sick I've been feeling. In fact, we wanted to talk to you children about it this week."

Collette felt chills racing up and down her

spine. What did her mother mean? Daddy already *knew* she was sick? So sick her parents wanted to gather everyone together and talk about it? Collette felt dizzy herself all of a sudden, thinking of the worst, most terrible diseases her mother might have right this minute.

"Oh, Mom," said Collette, trying to be brave, but ending up being just plain scared. "You're all right, aren't you? You're not going to die!"

Mrs. Murphy looked stricken herself for a second. Then she broke into a smile and reached down to hug Collette tightly. "Oh, no, of course not. I'm fine, Collette." Her mother patted her on the back. Next she laughed. "In fact, I'm better than fine; I'm pregnant!"

Chapter Three

"Pregnant?" Collette gasped as though her mother had just tossed a bucket of icy cold water in her face. "But . . . but you *can't* be pregnant!"

Mrs. Murphy grinned. "Yes, I can. I *am*, almost three months. I know it's a surprise, Collette. Gosh, I was a little surprised myself, but Daddy and I are thrilled."

Collette looked at her mother's face. Even with the ice pack and watery eyes, she was positively beaming.

Collette hopped off the bed and quickly closed the door. "But, Mom . . ." She lowered her voice. "No offense, but don't you think you're a *little old* to be having a baby? A second-grade teacher at school is pregnant and she's only twenty-two."

Mrs. Murphy slowly lowered her ice pack. "I am *not* too old, Collette. I'm only thirty-five."

"Thirty-five!" Collette shook her head. Thirty-five sounded a whole lot older than twenty-two!

Mrs. Murphy laughed and hugged Collette. "Honey, I thought you would be thrilled with the news. You love babies. When Aunt Michelle comes to visit, you carry Jesse all over the place."

Collette nodded. She did love babies, a lot. But the nice part about holding babies that didn't live in your house was that you could return them when they got in the way or their diaper smelled. A full-time, live-in baby would always be around. A live-in baby might start crying in the middle of a funny show or burp up formula all over a brand-new outfit. Collette drew in a deep breath, trying to digest the news. Just when Stevie had finally stopped *acting* like a big baby, another one was on the way. Collette shuddered. What if the new baby was another Stevie? Stevie was cute and a lot of fun, but he had tried to bite people until he was three, and he still had the loudest voice in the world. Whenever Collette had friends over, Stevie insisted on barging into her room to show

14

off. Stevie would probably teach the new baby all of his look-at-me tricks.

When Collette looked up, she saw the disappointed look in her mother's eyes. "Things won't be as crazy with this baby, Collette," her mother promised. "Remember, you were barely six years old when we brought Stevie home." Her mother laughed. "Stevie's five now. Time passes so quickly. We'll all enjoy this baby."

Collette nodded. Things *had* been crazy when Stevie was a baby, but kind of a nice crazy. Maybe her mother was right. Maybe this new baby would be a little girl that Collette and Laura could dress up and . . .

Collette's heart leapt as she glanced toward the door, thinking of her bedroom down the hall. If the baby was a girl, where would she sleep? They only had three bedrooms on the second floor, and the third floor was still stuffed with boxes of summer clothes, Christmas trains, and extra mattresses. Mrs. Murphy had promised Collette she would clean it out before spring. "You will have your own bedroom by your birthday, May fifteenth," she had announced last August. "Turning twelve is old enough for some privacy."

Now her mother was pregnant. She wouldn't be able to lift heavy boxes and drag mattresses downstairs for the Salvation Army. The third floor would probably have to wait till the baby was in kindergarten, maybe even first grade. By then Collette would be in high school!

Collette was about to suggest that the new baby sleep in a cradle in her parents' room, but she didn't. Her mother looked so tired. And besides, Collette didn't have to hear it to know. If the baby was a girl, the crib would go right next to Collette's bunk bed. The changing table would probably go in the hall by her door and a little night-light with clowns and balloons would shine right into Collette's face all night long.

With the weight of the sudden news, Collette could barely stand up. Her stomach churned. Was morning sickness contagious? She glanced down at her mother, glad to see her eyes closing, and covered her up with the soft plaid blanket.

Just think . . . in six months there would be *five* Murphy kids, living in the same house with the same two parents. Collette walked downstairs and into the warm small kitchen. She looked around, her heart sinking with the realization that

16

a high chair would never fit. They would have to start eating all their meals in the large dining room. Maybe they would all fit in there with the playpen and the musical windup swing. It wouldn't surprise Collette if her mother asked her to please *not* invite friends over during the baby's naptime for the next two years. And babies napped a lot.

Collette looked up and caught her reflection in the upper oven door. She looked as mean and selfish as she felt. Her cheeks burned. What was she thinking? Poor little baby, he hadn't done anything and his big sister already resented him. Hot, shameful tears stung her eyes.

The kitchen window rattled from the force of a snowball! Collette jumped. Had Stevie sneaked outside without his coat again? In December Stevie often pretended to be a polar bear and refused to wear anything but his fake Halloween teeth.

Before Collette could rush to the window, she saw Marsha's face pressed against it. Marsha crossed her eyes and held up a long icicle.

Collette laughed and hurried to the back door. Marsha was so funny. She lived across the street in the biggest house on the block. Too bad Marsha's mother wasn't the pregnant mom. Since Marsha was an only child, her parents had at least four bedrooms they weren't using.

"Hi. Boy, is it cold out there." Marsha pulled off her hat and sat on the bench and kicked off her boots. "Listen, I can only stay a second, but I came over to find out if you can go on Saturday. My mom just told me my aunt from St. Bede's is going to help out, and she'll promise to keep an eye on you. That should make you mom feel better." Marsha blew on her hands and stuck one under each armpit. "So how is your mom feeling anyway? My mom said she will probably feel better tomorrow."

Collette felt the lump in her throat grow to the size of a peach pit. "Well, I don't think my mom is going to feel well for a long time, Marsha."

Marsha's eyes bugged out. "Oh, no!" Even though Marsha was always complaining because Mrs. Murphy wouldn't let her put her feet on the furniture or drink the last of the milk, Collette knew Marsha really liked her mother. "When *will* she feel better? My mom said it was a twenty-four-hour flu. Is it the forty-eight-hour type?"

Collette shook her head as she slid onto the bench next to Marsha. "No. It's more like . . . the nine-month type . . . like a baby!"

"What?" Marsha shot up as if the news had injected her with rocket fuel. "*A baby?* Hey, you don't mean a real, live, get pregnant, go to the hospital and bring home a baby, do you?"

Collette nodded, searching Marsha's face. Maybe if Marsha broke into a huge smile and said, "Whoa — that's great!" Collette would think so, too. But Marsha's cheeks blazed red and she just kept blinking like she must be hearing things.

"A baby! Gosh — I never thought your mom would have *another* baby. I mean . . . you already have so many!"

"That's why my mom is so sick. Morning sickness."

Marsha leaned over and shook her head. "Yeah, but she got sick this afternoon."

Collette sighed, not sure why her mom was off schedule. Maybe it was because she was thirty-five years old instead of twenty-two.

"So . . ." Marsha whistled through her teeth. "Man-oh-man, does your dad know yet?"

"Of course he does, Marsha. But listen, don't tell anyone else because my brothers and Laura don't even know yet."

Marsha nodded. She looked around the kitchen and then lowered her voice. "Hey — maybe you shouldn't tell the kids at school until you *have* to."

"Why?" Collette knew lots of families at Sacred Heart who had five or six kids. Sacred Heart even gave you a discount on tuition after three kids.

Marsha shifted in her seat. "Well, no offense, but having *five kids* is not really the all-American thing to do anymore. Nobody is going to come up and pat you on the back or anything. This new baby will be using disposable diapers that are bad for the environment, and his formula will come in those cans that your mom never gets around to recycling, and when he grows up and gets married, he may have six kids and that makes seven more kids your parents added to this crowded world." Marsha jabbed her elbow into Collette's side. "And what if all seven of them use aerosol hair spray. That's going to blow a huge hole in the ozone layer all right. I bet your mom never thought of that!"

Collette leaned back against the bench, her

head beginning to pound. Gosh, she had only been worried about her crowded bedroom. Now she had to worry about the effect this baby was going to have on the whole world!

"So did your parents ask you kids to vote on having another baby?" Marsha was sitting up straight like she was conducting an interview for 20/20. "I mean, since your dad announced he is allergic to dogs, was this second choice?"

"Well, of *course not*, Marsha." Collette felt her cheeks growing warm. She could tell from talking to her mother that this baby had been a surprise, but her parents loved kids! Just because Marsha lived so close, she thought she could ask these none-of-your-business questions whenever she wanted. "You don't vote on babies."

Marsha bent down and jammed her feet into her boots. "Well, that's a little rude, don't you think? I mean, a new baby can mess up a lot of things!" She grabbed her scarf and swung it around her neck. "I'm not even going to ask if you can go skiing on Saturday. With another baby on the way, you'll be scrubbing floors or doing laundry. Face it, Collette. This baby means you're going to be a permanent second mother around here for the next four or five years." Marsha zipped up her jacket and scowled. "I can't believe you guys are having *another* baby."

"Marsha! Are you mad about this baby or something?"

Marsha shook back her black hair and pulled down her ski hat. "Of course not. I don't have to live over here with crying babies and little jars of runny baby food filling up the whole refrigerator. As your friend, I am just feeling sorry for you, that's all. See you!"

As the door slammed, Collette went to the window and watched as Marsha stomped off through the shifting snow. Hearing her own bitter words coming from Marsha's mouth made Collette feel even worse. Marsha's predictions about the baby sounded so mean and selfish. Worse yet, what if they turned out to be true?

Chapter Four

Marsha was still offering her opinions on Mrs. Murphy's pregnancy on the school bus the next morning. "My mother almost died when I told her the news about your mom. I had to repeat it three times before she believed me. Even my dad thought it was an early April Fools' joke or something. My mother is so great, though. She just smiled and said, 'Well, what's done is done and let's just hope they can pull it off.' My mom thinks you should start redecorating the third floor as soon as possible. And, she hopes that Stevie doesn't regress or anything since everyone thought he was going to be the baby forever. A new, unexpected baby can really mess up a little kid's mind. My aunt is a psychologist, though, in case Stevie starts sucking his thumb again. We might be able to get you a discount." Marsha grinned at Collette and giggled. "My dad is so funny. He said a cocker spaniel would have been a whole lot cheaper and much easier to paper train!"

"Marsha!" Collette flopped back against the bus seat. "I told you *not* to tell anyone. My parents just told the other kids this morning. This is private news."

Marsha gripped Collette's arm. "How did they take it? Did anyone cry? Does Stevie want to run away?"

Collette almost growled. Marsha was acting like her parents were trying to *break up* the family instead of just add to it. "Everyone, especially Stevie, was very happy. *We are all very happy about the baby!*"

Collette heard how mechanical her last sentence sounded, like she was trying to convince herself to *be* happy. She leaned her head against the bus window and sighed, wishing her feelings were as uncomplicated as her brothers' and Laura's. When *they* heard the news, they started clapping. They were all so young and . . . maybe nicer. They didn't ask a lot of selfish questions, like where the baby was going to sleep and where the high chair would fit in the small kitchen. The other kids just reacted to the wonderfulness of a new baby. Stevie even ran upstairs to get his old blanket for the baby to keep.

Collette looked outside the bus window at the white hillside, staring at the bare trees with their penciled branches outlined black against the snow. Somehow, her mixed-up, selfish feelings seemed out of place. Why was she dwelling on all the ripples the baby was going to create instead of the baby itself?

"So is your mom going to do that amnio-census test?" asked Marsha. "My mom says it's practically a *law* that you have to have it if you're over thirty-two."

"What are you talking about?" Collette was getting a little mad that Marsha and her mother knew so much more about Mrs. Murphy's pregnancy than she did.

"This amnio-census — or whatever it's called, test . . . tells you that the baby is okay." Marsha poked Collette in the side with her elbow. "My mom said your mom is a little old to keep having babies . . . no offense. My mom was twenty-six when she had me."

"My mother is still young, Marsha," exploded Collette. "She is two years younger than *your* mom."

Marsha flipped her dark hair back over her shoulder and shrugged. "Well, my mom isn't throwing up and being pregnant, is she?"

Collette was about to say something back when she noticed how upset Marsha looked. Except for the large red blotches growing on each cheek, Marsha's face was as white as snow. Collette turned away. Why should Marsha be mad about anything? She had the most perfect life in the world. Not only was she an only child, but her parents both adored her to death. Collette could still remember back in the second grade when Marsha was scheduled to read one sentence during a school Mass. It had been a simple, "Let us pray for the sick of the parish," but her parents had sat in the front pew beaming like she had just opened on Broadway. And then afterwards they gave Marsha a rose and took her picture in front of the Blessed Mary statue. Months later when Collette was chosen to carry up the gifts during the Christmas Mass her mother had had to leave early because Stevie wouldn't stop trying to crawl into the manger scene to hug baby Jesus. Collette felt another sting of doubt. With a brand-new baby in the house, her parents would probably have to miss a lot of Collette's school events.

As soon as the bus stopped, Collette got off and hurried across the playground. Since her mother still didn't feel well, a sitter was scheduled to come right before lunch to take care of Stevie when he got off the kindergarten van.

This morning the snow had been falling so heavily, Mr. Murphy had left before seven to avoid bumper-to-bumper traffic. The whole morning had been pretty crazy. Stevie had thrown his red boots out the bathroom window to make Jeff laugh. Collette tried putting them in the dryer, but they made so much noise clunking around and around she finally took them out and made Stevie wear Laura's. That meant Laura had to wear Jeff's and Jeff had to wear Collette's, which made him really mad. By that time Collette could see that her mother just wanted to go back to bed, so she just rammed her feet into her mother's boots, which were two or three sizes too large for Collette.

Because of the bitterly cold weather, everyone was allowed in the school building early. Collette bent her head down against the gusting wind and hurried to catch up with Sarah, her best friend since third grade. She wanted to talk to her privately about this whole pregnancy business. Sarah was so kind and logical. She would know exactly the right thing to say to make Collette realize that having another brother or sister was probably the greatest thing in the world. Collette caught up with Sarah by the lockers. Telling her would be kind of exciting, actually. She could hardly wait to see the expression on her face. But as soon as Sarah turned around, she reached out and hugged Collette. "Oh, Collette, congratulations! I can't believe your mom is having another baby!"

"What? Who told you?" Before she could even close her mouth, Collette saw Marsha running up to a group of girls and talking a mile a minute. Collette watched as the girls started to laugh and turned to stare at Collette.

"I just can't believe it!" Sarah cried. "You are

so lucky. I sure wish *my* mom would have another baby."

Collette kicked off her mother's boots and pulled off her blue ski hat. "I wanted to tell you, privately. I wish Marsha would stop blabbing this to the whole school."

Sarah laughed. "Well, you know Marsha. She likes to be the first one to break a story."

Collette slammed her locker. "Yeah, well this story is *my life*. I really don't want the whole world to know my mom is pregnant."

Sarah nudged Collette with her shoulder. "Why not? It's great news." Sarah reached out and squeezed Collette's arm. "Is everything okay? I hope your mom isn't still sick. Is that why you want to keep it a secret? Till your mom feels better."

Instantly Collette felt ashamed again. Somewhere deep inside her she must not like the idea of a baby at all. Why else would she keep erupting with such mean thoughts? Collette shifted her book bag, feeling so awful she didn't even want to look up at Sarah. Too bad it wasn't Sarah's mom having the baby. It would have been a luckier baby, coming into a family with a loving big sister.

"Okay, girls, time to pay the piper!" Roger poked his Bic pen into Collette's back. "There are only twenty more seats on the second activity bus for the ski trip, Collette. Should I mark you down or will you be going by private limo this trip?" Roger wiggled his eyebrows up and down and grinned. "For an additional dollar I can guarantee a seat next to me."

Sarah groaned and rolled her eyes. "Save the sales pitch. Collette isn't allowed to go, Roger."

Roger looked disappointed. He poked Collette in the shoulder with his clipboard. "Hey, Murphy, why not? Everyone is going. You can sit next to me for free."

Collette smiled. Roger was kind of a goof most of the time, but he was really funny and nice. She almost wished she could explain what was going on with her family, but decided against it. You never knew how boys were going to take personal stuff.

"Sarah, I really have to talk to you at lunch," whispered Collette as soon as Roger dove into another crowd. "My mom is so sick, and . . ."

"Did she throw up some more?" Sarah looked worried.

"About six more times. My grandmother is coming home early from her vacation if my mom isn't better by Monday."

The bell rang, and Mr. Kurtlander grinned and waved the rest of the kids still in the hall into the classroom. "Hurry up, class. Watch the wet floor. Greg, go get the mop, buddy."

As Collette walked past, Mr. Kurtlander tapped her gently on the head with his papers. "Hey, congratulations. Marsha just told me Murphy number five is on the way."

Collette looked up at Mr. Kurtlander and nodded. Holy cow — Marsha was a regular Paul Revere! By lunchtime, the entire school plus the retired nuns living in the convent next door would all know the news. Mrs. Murphy was pregnant!

"Hey, we're still two ahead of you!" laughed Erin Freyvogel from the desk beside her. "We have *five* girls and two boys!" Erin made a face. "The boys make the most noise, though."

Collette managed to smile back. Erin was one of the friendliest and nicest girls in the class. She was always laughing about something. Her mother still helped at school, driving for lots of field trips. Even with seven kids, Erin's mom acted exactly the same way she always did. Collette leaned back in her seat. Her mom would probably still volunteer. Maybe her parents would trade their old blue station wagon and get a fancy new van. Maybe a bright red van with high back seats. Families with five kids needed special cars. Once Collette saw a van with a television built in. That would be perfect. Then the new baby could watch *Sesame Street* while her mom drove back and forth on car pools. Collette smiled. Who said that having another baby meant things had to get worse? Maybe things would even get better! What was so terrible about sharing a bedroom with a baby for a year or two? Just this morning, her dad told her that he was going to start cleaning out the third floor as soon as he finished his Ohio court case. He drew a sketch right on his napkin and said that they might even add a skylight so Collette could watch the stars at night.

Collette smiled, suddenly thinking of how much fun it would be to show a brand-new baby a star for the first time. She reached inside her desk, pulled out her yellow tablet, flipped it open, and started printing names in two straight columns, boys on the left, girls on the right. "Patricia, Re-

becca, Billy, Tommy, Rhodora, Susannah . . ."
Collette chewed on her eraser and smiled. Those
were great names, but she wanted to think of the
best name in the world for this baby. Maybe even
a name with a hyphen . . . Emily-Alexandria. John-
Paul. This baby deserved a fancy name. Since he
was at the bottom of a five-kid totem pole, he
would get lots of hand-me-downs and have to go
to hundreds of school concerts and open houses
before he even started kindergarten. At least his
name should be brand new. Collette would present her mother with the list as soon as she got
home from school today. Her mother would love
it. The whole family could vote on a name right
after dinner. This new baby was going to be the
best family project yet.

Chapter Five

There were fifteen girl's names and ten boy's names on Collette's list by the time the school bus stopped at her street.

"I like Melissa-Maria best!" Marsha's chin had been digging into Collette's shoulder the whole bus trip. "But definitely Peter Orrington if it's a boy."

Collette looked down at her list and then up at Marsha. "What? That's not on the list. Where did you get Orrington?"

Marsha's face turned deep red. "My great-grandmother's name was Orrington."

Collette smiled. "Well, it's a great name, Marsha, but I don't know if my parents want to name

34

their baby after one of *your* relatives."

"She was very rich, Collette. My mom has this fifty-foot tray with a giant O right in the middle. We could give your baby that for a christening present."

Collette was glad that Marsha wasn't acting mad anymore about her mom being pregnant. Maybe after telling all the kids in the school about Mrs. Murphy and seeing how happy they were, Marsha realized that the baby was pretty exciting news after all. Collette grabbed her book bag and stood up, anxious to run in and show her mother the list of baby names.

Because the snow had drifted so deep on the driveway, Jeff and Collette had to pull Laura up to the side door.

"If it keeps snowing, my teacher said school will be closed for tomorrow," said Laura. "I hope not 'cause I'm still making my valentine box. I brought it home to fix up. It won't snow on Valentine's Day, will it, Collette?"

"I hope not."

"Oh, yeah. I have to take in two dozen cookies for Valentine's Day," said Jeff. "Do you think Mom will be able to bake some?"

Collette kicked away the snow blocking the side door and pulled it open. "Probably. Maybe she's out of bed now."

She pulled off her boots and set them on the braided rug. The house was unusually dark and quiet, except for the television blaring from the downstairs game room. Collette walked into the kitchen. Her mother must still be resting. Their usual after-school snack was not waiting for them on the kitchen table. Maybe their sitter didn't have kids of her own and didn't realize how hungry children got after school. Collette opened a kitchen cabinet and pulled out a bag of potato chips and a box of raisins. "Jeff, pour some milk. I'll be right back."

Before she even got all the way downstairs, Collette heard Stevie laughing. She peeked around the corner and saw the sitter grinning at him. "I can't believe you think this is funny, Stevie," she said. The sitter was in her early twenties. She shook back her hair and pointed to the television set. "Now this guy with the dark hair, Brad, is dating Felicia, the blonde babe."

Stevie was sitting next to the sitter, nodding his head.

36

"Oh — look at that Brad. Now . . . here comes the good part," said the sitter. "That blonde lady is a real sneak. She never tells the truth. She lied yesterday and told all her friends that she's having a baby."

"My mom is having a baby," said Stevie. "But she's throwing up."

The sitter checked her watch. "I know, I've been running up and down the steps so much I've missed half of my shows. Listen, your brother and sisters are due home so I'd better check. You stay here and tell me what the blonde says to Brad, okay?"

"I'll come with you!" cried Stevie.

Collette barely had time to turn around before the sitter and Stevie raced up.

"Oh, hi," the sitter said cheerfully. "I'm Debbie. You must be Collette. Did your brother and sister get off the bus?"

"They're in the kitchen. I got them a snack."

"Great, thanks a lot. Stevie and I kinda lost track of time, watching television."

"Debbie doesn't care how much TV I watch," added Stevie. "She says it's good dusty action."

Collette and Debbie gave each other a puzzled

look. Finally Debbie laughed. "Not *dusty* action, kiddo. I said television was a good *distraction*, Stevie."

Debbie grabbed Stevie and tickled him under the arms. "You are so cute, buster."

"How's my mother feeling?" Collette asked loudly. She could tell Stevie was having a great time with the sitter, but she really didn't know if the sitter was supposed to be having so much fun with Stevie.

Debbie flipped back her thick reddish ponytail and sighed.

"Oh, gosh, she wasn't feeling too hot today. Want to run her up some ginger ale, Collette?"

Collette nodded, watching as Debbie flung Stevie over her shoulder and carried him back downstairs. "Stevie and me have to check on Brad, right, Kiddo?"

"Brad needs *more space*," Stevie said seriously.

Collette practically ran into the kitchen, grabbing a can of ginger ale and a box of crackers. With Debbie busy downstairs with her soap opera, no telling how long her mother had been ignored upstairs, all by herself. Collette added a glass with ice to the tray and tossed on two oatmeal cookies.

38

The tray clattered and jingled as she hurried upstairs. Her mother's bedroom door was partially closed, so Collette stuck her foot in and pushed it open.

Her mother smiled as soon as Collette walked in. "Hi, honey. How was school? Any news?"

Collette felt better having her mother ask the same old questions she always did when she came home from school. "Fine. Except Marsha told the whole school you're pregnant. Mr. Kurtlander thinks Daddy is trying for his own football squad."

Mrs. Murphy's small smile only lasted a second. "Well, this baby is a linebacker, that's for sure. He sure is causing problems. I'm not allowed to go downstairs until Monday."

Collette nearly dropped the tray. She pushed aside the lamp and set it down. "Oh, no. Should I call the doctor?"

Mrs. Murphy smiled and reached out for Collette's hand. "No, I already did and he thinks bed rest is all I need. I just keep thinking of all the work piling up downstairs. Did Debbie remember to take out the tuna casserole and unload the dishwasher?"

Collette shrugged, deciding against telling her

mother that Debbie probably hadn't. She had probably been too busy explaining the love lives of everyone on the afternoon soaps to Stevie to stop and unload glasses and mismatched spoons.

"How long will Debbie be baby-sitting?" Collette tried to keep her voice light, so her mother wouldn't think anything was wrong.

"Till the end of the week. I go back to the doctor on Monday morning."

Collette nodded. "Well, here's your tray. I guess I'd better hurry downstairs and make sure Stevie is okay."

Collette's hand flew to her mouth at the same moment her mother's eyebrows went up. "Isn't Debbie still downstairs?"

Collette smiled, trying a cheerful laugh so her mother wouldn't get upset. "Oh, sure, yeah . . . she's down in the game room with Stevie right now."

Mrs. Murphy kept one eyebrow up. "Is everything all right, Collette?"

"Oh, sure, fine. Great!"

By the time Collette had convinced her mother that Debbie was practically teaching Stevie how to multiply and divide, she had a splitting headache. Actually she wasn't sure if her little brother should be downstairs watching the afternoon soap operas. It would make Collette feel a whole lot better when her mother was able to come downstairs and turn *Sesame Street* back on. Big Bird made a lot more sense than Brad and the soaps ever could. The news of a brand-new baby in the Murphy house seemed to flip everything into different gear. Collette bit her lip. Maybe it was a gear too fast to handle!

Chapter Six

That night, Stevie made Debbie three valentine cards after dinner. He also made a large heart for Brad.

"Daddy, mail this one to television." Stevie held out his card and grinned.

Collette thought her father would be angry when Stevie finished explaining how he and Debbie watched the soaps all afternoon. But Mr. Murphy just laughed.

"Don't worry, Collette," he said after Stevie and the other kids left the room. "A few days of soap shows won't scar him. At least he's happy and he's not bothering your mother. That's the most important thing right now." His face grew serious as he bent to load the dishwasher. "Your mother needs her rest."

"Is Mom going to be all right?" asked Collette. Her mother didn't come down for dinner, and the doctor had called from the hospital to see how she was feeling. Only doctors in old movies called patients when they were really worried.

"Sure, sure, she's going to be just fine." But he didn't smile at Collette like he really meant it. Instead, he held onto a handful of dripping silverware and stared outside at the snow for a long time.

"Did Mom have to stay in bed a lot when she was pregnant with me?"

"No, not with any of you. But every pregnancy is different and sometimes, if a baby isn't strong enough, well . . ."

"Sometimes what?"

Daddy let the silverware fall back into the soapy water.

"Sometimes a baby starts to grow, but then . . ." Collette could tell her father was searching for the right words. That scared Collette, reminding her of when he had searched for the right words last summer to tell her her granddad's cancer had come back.

"Is our baby strong enough to keep growing?"

Mr. Murphy put his arm around Collette and gave it a squeeze. "I hope so. But your mother is having some problems and I guess I need you to help the baby-sitters as much as you can. Your mother is not to get out of bed or there is a chance she may *lose* the baby."

Lose the baby . . . Collette suddenly felt icy-cold inside. Her mother couldn't lose the baby now. Collette swallowed hard. Her mother couldn't lose the baby now that Collette finally *wanted* it. Collette felt something sour in her mouth and wondered if guilt had a taste. Maybe God was trying to teach Collette a lesson about being selfish. As soon as she thought about it, Collette knew God didn't work that way. But she felt responsible anyway. She should have hugged her mother the moment she heard the news.

"Daddy!" Laura hurried into the room, her face stricken. "Hurry up!"

Mr. Murphy dropped a platter onto the counter. "What's wrong? Is Mommy sick again?"

Laura shook her head and grabbed onto his hand, pulling him toward the hall. "No, but Debbie just called. She told Stevie her car got broken and she can't come to baby-sit him anymore. Stevie is crying his head off."

Collette watched her father hurry out of the room. She looked down at the broken platter. Five large pieces were scattered across the counter. It was the pink poppy design; her mother's favorite. Collette frowned, wondering if she would be able to glue the pieces together again. She took the last glass out of the sink and watched the water empty down the drain, then took a napkin and wiped out the leftover bubbles and shined the counters one last time. If her mother were to walk in right now she would be proud of the shiny kitchen. It looked clean and bright, like a kitchen in an ad for cereal or oven cleaner. Even though everything was in its place, Collette knew something was *out* of place. Her mother. She belonged in the kitchen, helping Laura with her valentine box, or downstairs with Stevie so he wouldn't need Debbie anymore. Suddenly Collette missed her mother so much! It seemed like she was in Alaska instead of upstairs in bed.

Even with Stevie crying in the next room and Jeff and Laura fighting over the TV, the house seemed too quiet. Collette turned off the kitchen light. If only her mom would stay in bed till Gramma came on Monday, things would be fine. On Monday, the little baby would be six days stronger and six days bigger.

By Monday, the sour taste in Collette's mouth would disappear and the awful fears about the baby would fade.

Collette put her hand on the banister and listened for her mother. But all she could hear was her heartbeat, getting faster and louder. The baby had to be all right. Collette already had twenty-five names picked out. The whole school was excited about the news. The Murphys really wanted the baby. Collette felt her eyes sting. She wanted the baby, too. What if none of that was enough?

Chapter Seven

The new sitter, Mrs. Warren, arrived at seven o'clock the next morning.

As soon as Collette took her coat, Mrs. Warren tied on a starched apron and started to work. She made the coffee, set out the juice and cereal bowls, and got out her notepad.

"Now, with the snow, your father left early so you'll have to fill me in on a few details." Mrs. Warren smiled at Collette, but she kept tapping her pencil on her pad like she would appreciate the facts as quickly as Collette could produce them. "Ages and names of children," asked Mrs. Warren. "You first."

Collette cleared her throat and stood up a little

straighter. "I'm Collette, age eleven, Jeff is nine, Laura is seven, and Stevie is five."

Mrs. Warren glanced up, alarmed. "There are four of you? The agency said *three* children. Three is my limit."

Collette shrugged. "Well, three of us will be in school till three-thirty, and Stevie is only here half the day."

Mrs. Warren started to smile again. "Well, I'm sure things will be just fine. Now sit down and eat, dear. I'll hurry up the others. The roads are icy and I don't want to have to drive anyone to school if they miss the bus."

Collette slid into her seat, hoping everyone had found missing socks and book bags. Mrs. Warren seemed nice, but she did keep her notebook in her hand as she marched upstairs. Collette had the feeling she was going to write down anything that was off schedule.

Breakfast was quiet. Stevie kept staring at Mrs. Warren over his juice glass. Jeff and Laura didn't even fight over the ball that slid into Laura's cereal bowl. Laura just set it in the center of the table and everyone stared at it till Mrs. Warren dusted the frosted-flake sugar from it and put it on the counter.

"Now, I will expect Steven at eleven-thirty, and the rest of you at three-thirty. Is that correct?" Mrs. Warren smiled at everyone. Collette knew there was no reason for them to feel so shy around her. Maybe it was because Daddy explained she was from an agency. Maybe it was because she was wearing white. Collette chewed her frosted flakes thoughtfully. Maybe it was because they all missed their mother.

Halfway to the bus stop, Stevie started to cry. Huge, fat tears rolled down his cheeks. Even Jeff, who usually got embarrassed whenever Stevie caused a scene in public, put his arm around Stevie. It was as if Stevie were crying for all of them.

"I don't want to come home to that nurse lady all by myself," Stevie whimpered. "Can I stay in school with you big guys?"

Laura looked up at Collette hopefully. "I could use him for show and tell."

Jeff groaned. "No way. Sister Mary Elizabeth checks the van to make sure the kindergarten kids are all on." Jeff elbowed Stevie. "Hey, don't worry. Mom is still upstairs."

"The sitter told me I wasn't allowed to bother Mommy," cried Stevie.

"Mrs. Warren is nice, Stevie," reminded Collette. "I saw her put that bouncing ball in your snack bag. You can play with it on the bus. And *I'll* play with you when I get home from school. We'll play Candy Land, okay?"

"Okay!" Stevie smiled. "Thanks, Collette."

Collette saw the bus as it rounded the corner. "Come on, guys." She didn't want to have to walk back to the house and tell Mrs. Warren they'd missed it. "Stevie, I have money, so I'll call you from school during lunch, okay? I'll call and you can tell me what you are doing with the nurse — I mean, baby-sitter. Okay?"

Stevie grinned. "You mean you'll call *just me*?"

Collette pulled him along by the arm, hurrying as the yellow lights started to flash on the school bus. "Sure. And Marsha and Sarah will say hi, too. How about that?"

Stevie broke free and started to race toward the bus. "That's real good, Collette. Hey, Marsha. You're going to call just me on the phone today."

Collette bent her head down and ran faster. Marsha loved Stevie so she would enjoy the call. Collette would like it, too. It would give her a chance to talk to Stevie and to make sure her mother was still okay. The bedroom door had been closed when they left the house. It was the first time Collette had not been able to say good-bye to her mother before she left for school. She looked up ahead at Stevie. Being five was nice. You were able to cry whenever you wanted and people didn't think you were nuts. Being eleven was a lot harder. You had to pretend things were fine, even when they weren't.

By the time the school bus pulled onto Walnut Street, Stevie and Laura were already laughing with their friends. Collette turned around and looked at Jeff. He looked pretty miserable. Collette knew her brother tried to be tough all the time, but she was going to have to talk to him sometime today. He knew something funny was going on. Last night while they were all brushing their teeth, he stopped, his mouth all foaming white, and just stared in the mirror. "Hey, Collette," he had said, lowering his voice. "Sister Miriam said if a baby isn't baptized, and then he dies, he goes to limbo. He never gets to go up to heaven."

Collette had nodded. Sister Miriam had told her the same thing in fourth grade.

"Well, that isn't fair. How can we baptize our baby inside Mom? I mean, what if he dies before he comes out?" Jeff had added.

Collette shivered, remembering how helpless she had felt. She didn't have an answer. Maybe God had special rules for babies still growing. Better yet, God probably took all babies back into heaven, no matter what.

Collette walked Stevie into his kindergarten class, even though she hadn't done that since he started in September. She even walked past Laura's second-grade classroom and then Jeff's class before she walked upstairs. Now that her mother was sick, she felt sort of protective. She almost felt like Gramma's cocker spaniel, a dog who never bothered to bark except when Granddad was away.

Collette walked up the worn marble stairs, wishing she could feel the way she had last week, before she knew what she knew now. Last week she would have been worried about the math quiz or Marsha ignoring her for no reason. Today, those worries seemed dumb; they didn't count as much. For some reason, worrying about her mom and the new baby made Collette feel older, but sadder. The same way she had felt when she found out there wasn't a Santa Claus after all.

Chapter Eight

That afternoon, school was dismissed an hour early because of the snow. Everyone was laughing and very excited on the bus ride home.

"The ski trip is going to be so great," laughed Marsha. "I heard that a parent from Cathedral used to be a real ski instructor and he is coming up to give free lessons. Roger said he was going to try and go down the hill on only one ski."

Collette laughed. Roger would probably do a good job of it, too. He wasn't afraid of anything except math.

"So, I guess since your mom is sick there's no chance of you going skiing at Seven Springs, is there?" asked Marsha. Collette was glad to see how disappointed Marsha looked. At least Sarah and Marsha would miss her.

"No. I don't want to even ask again." Collette picked up her book bag as the bus slowed for her stop. Actually, it was funny but Collette didn't *want* to go skiing anymore. The most important thing right now was getting her mom better, not getting on the bus for Seven Springs.

"Well, this snow will make the skiing even better," said Marsha. "My mother is so funny. Last night she gave me special heat packets to stick in my boots. I don't know where she finds this stuff!"

"Talk to you later, Marsha," called Collette as she got off the bus and hurried down the sidewalk. She caught up with Jeff and Laura by the driveway. "Wait up, guys!"

"Look at all this snow!" laughed Laura. "Let's build a snow fort."

Jeff looked around the front yard. "I wonder why Stevie hasn't even started a snowman yet. He must be sick."

Collette hurried inside. Stevie loved the snow. He usually had at least three snowmen standing at attention by the pine trees. Maybe he *was* sick.

The game room was as quiet as the rest of the house. No television set, no radio.

"Maybe they went to see a movie," suggested Laura. "To make Mommy feel better."

Collette sat down on the bottom step and yanked off both boots, then hurried into the kitchen. Mrs. Warren looked up from her coffee and magazine and smiled.

"Oh, hello. I didn't expect you for another hour."

Collette glanced around the spotless kitchen. "Where's Stevie?"

Mrs. Warren grinned and pointed upstairs with her index finger. "He's taking a little nap. He protested, but I thought he needed it. I was just about to wake him up and give him a snack."

"Stevie's taking a nap?" Collette couldn't believe it. Even when Stevie had the flu, he stayed awake until his parents forced him to go to sleep. Stevie didn't want to miss a minute of being alive.

Jeff and Laura walked into the kitchen. Both of them stared at the empty table. Day two of no snack waiting for them.

Mrs. Warren bent down and looked out the window. "Gosh, this snow is really coming down. I hope my plane won't be delayed."

"What plane?" asked Collette. Surely Mrs. Warren wasn't deserting them. It was only Wednesday! Mrs. Murphy wasn't allowed out of bed until Monday.

Mrs. Warren turned around and smiled. "Good news! My daughter had her second baby this afternoon, Sharon Michelle. She arrived two weeks early and I'm flying to Chicago tonight to take care of my grandson, Nicky."

"But *my* mom and *her* baby have to stay in bed," reminded Collette. "What are we going to do about tomorrow?"

Mrs. Warren looked concerned, but Collette could tell she was already thinking about what she was going to fix her grandson for dinner tomorrow.

"The agency. They have lots of sitters available. I already called. I'm sure they will send somebody else tomorrow morning." Mrs. Warren checked her notepad. "I have to wake Steven and check on your mother. Why don't you get yourself a snack and start your homework?"

Laura and Jeff exchanged horrified looks. Their

mother *never* made them do homework the moment they got home. She always wanted them to unwind after doing schoolwork all day.

As soon as Mrs. Warren left the kitchen, Collette started to organize the snack. She poured some caramel corn into a bowl and got out a huge bottle of ginger ale. Jeff and Laura both grinned when Collette got out four fancy stemmed glasses and added a cherry to each one.

"Will the baby-sitter mind?" Jeff asked as Collette started to pour.

Collette shook her head, feeling very much in charge. "Why? It's our house. Besides, Mrs. Warren will be in Chicago tomorrow."

"Yeah," added Laura. "She won't be here helping me with my valentine box. I have to have it done by Friday, Collette. I keep making hearts that look like circles."

"And I still need somebody to bake all those cookies for my party on Friday," reminded Jeff. "If Mrs. Warren is going to be in Chicago who will be here taking care of us?"

"Don't worry," Collette said calmly. "We'll just have to tell the agency to send us a sitter who knows how to make great valentine hearts and delicious cookies."

"I hope they have someone like that," Laura said slowly. "Will Daddy have to pay extra?"

Collette plunked another cherry into Laura's glass and grinned. "Don't worry. Tomorrow's sitter will be the best one yet. I promise."

Chapter Nine

Collette followed Mrs. Warren into the kitchen and listened as the sitter called Mr. Murphy to let him know she was going to Chicago. "So I won't be coming here tomorrow to watch your kids 'cause my own family needs me right now." Collette heard her father's deep groan at the other end of the line as though somebody had just stabbed him.

After the deep groan, Mrs. Warren only stayed on the line for a few more minutes. Her neck got bright red and she told Mr. Murphy that she knew she was to work until Monday, but her granddaughter was early and that was that.

When Mr. Murphy got home, he paid Mrs. Warren and said a polite good-bye. But he didn't smile and he didn't touch one bite of his dinner. "The baby-sitting agency told me they were sorry about Mrs. Warren but they couldn't find me a replacement until next week." Collette stopped chewing and watched her father rub his hands over his eyes like he was having a hard time staying awake. He sat with the phone book on his lap and kept calling people to see if they could baby-sit.

"Daddy, I want *you* to baby-sit me," said Stevie. "I'm real good."

Mr. Murphy reached out and hugged Stevie. It was the first time he had smiled since he had walked in the door. "I know you are. But I have to be in court, bright and early."

"Let Stevie be one of the jury people, Dad," suggested Jeff.

Mr. Murphy grinned and started to dial again. He was trying neighbors now. Each one already had plans. Marsha's mother even offered to take Stevie with her to her garden club card party, but Mr. Murphy said no. "Thanks, but I need someone here in case Kate needs anything. She can't get out of bed until Monday."

At eight o'clock, Mr. Murphy got so desperate,

he started to call the elderly lady who lived in the dark house at the end of the street.

"I don't want the witch lady to watch me!" Stevie hid his face in his hands. "She eats cats!"

Mr. Murphy put down the phone and frowned. "She what?"

Jeff looked disgusted. "She doesn't eat cats, dummy. She eats dogs. And sometimes squirrels."

"One Thanksgiving she ate a raccoon, right, Jeff?" asked Laura. "But, Stevie, don't worry because she never eats kids."

Mr. Murphy leaned back in his chair and rubbed his hands over his eyes.

Collette tried to finish her homework, but she was too worried. What were they going to do?

"Hey, Dad, look at how much snow is coming down now," said Jeff. "And frost is growing inside the window. Maybe school will be canceled tomorrow. Maybe the courthouse will be closed, too."

"That would be great, Dad," Collette said brightly. "Then you could stay home and watch us."

Mr. Murphy got up from his chair, looking more worried than ever. He turned on the radio and fiddled with the knob until he got the news. "Let's listen, kids. I heard the temperature was really going to drop tomorrow. I hope school isn't canceled. What would I do with all of you?"

Stevie leaned against his father's leg. "Please don't send us to the witch lady."

"Even birds are afraid to fly over her yard," Laura added. "Even crows."

"Temperatures will reach an all-time low, tomorrow," the radio announcer warned. "Temperatures will be in the low teens with a wind chill of minus twenty. Tune in tomorrow for a list of school closings. . . ."

Jeff stood up and clapped. "Ya-hoo." He closed his math book and shoved it back inside his book bag.

"What am I going to do?" Mr. Murphy asked. "I still have to go to work."

The kitchen was so quiet Collette could hear the wind whistling up the driveway outside. Mr. Murphy picked up the phone and then put it down again. The agency didn't have anyone available, and he had run out of people to call.

Collette looked at Jeff, Laura, and Stevie. They were a little crazy at times, but not *that* much trouble. Why was it so hard to find a baby-sitter?

Mr. Murphy picked up the phone again. "Maybe I could call Aunt Michelle. I could drive up to Altoona to pick her up."

"Daddy, Aunt Michelle lives *two hours* away!" reminded Collette. "The roads are too bad."

Mr. Murphy sighed. "You're right." He gave Collette a tired smile. "Too bad you're not a little older, Collette. Then you could baby-sit. That would solve everything."

As soon as Collette heard the words, she knew it would work. Then Laura and Jeff started laughing and Stevie raced over and hugged Collette.

"I want Collette!" Stevie cried. "She won't call me Steven and make me take naps."

"Can I, Daddy?" asked Collette. It was a great plan. "I'll only be missing one day of school. I've only missed two days so far."

Mr. Murphy shook his head. "No. You're only eleven, peanut."

"But I watched the kids in the afternoon a couple of times for Mom," reminded Collette. "And I fixed them lunch."

Mr. Murphy started to look interested. "Your mother thought that was okay?"

Collette nodded. "She even paid me."

"Real money," added Stevie.

Mr. Murphy looked outside at the snow, then turned around to study Collette. Collette stood up straighter and shook back her hair. She was as tall as any thirteen-year-old. That had to count for something.

"Well . . . it is tempting, and I am fresh out of names."

"*Please*, Daddy. Mom will be right upstairs. And the kids will listen to me."

"We will," Jeff and Laura said at once.

Mr. Murphy looked down at Stevie. "Let me talk to your mother. Will you be real good for Collette? I don't want your mom to get out of bed all day."

Stevie nodded and took a step closer to Collette. "I will be so good you won't believe your eyes."

Collette put her arm around Stevie's shoulder and tried to look as grown up as she could. "Go upstairs and talk to Mom about it. She will tell you that I can handle it, Daddy. I really can. You won't have a thing to worry about."

Mr. Murphy reached out his hand and Collette shook it. She kept smiling until her father's worried expression disappeared. Tomorrow would be a snap. And maybe when her parents saw how well she took care of the kids and house, they would insist that she go to Seven Springs to ski and relax. After all, if she was grown up enough to watch three kids for ten hours, she was certainly grown up enough to ski down a hill.

Collette turned around and started clearing the table. She even got Jeff to help rinse and gave Stevie the broom to sweep up the crumbs. She wanted her father to see how well she could handle being in charge. Tomorrow would be the perfect chance to show her parents how grown-up she really was!

Chapter Ten

Collette turned off her alarm at six o'clock and tiptoed down into the dark kitchen. It was so cold outside, she could scrape ice from inside the drafty kitchen window. She turned on the light and flipped through the radio stations until she found the weather.

". . . with a wind chill factor of minus thirty-four. Bundle up if you *have* to go outside, but we suggest that you stay inside. Now for a complete list of school closings . . . Burrell Elementary, Cathedral High School, Copeland Academy . . ." Collette pulled out the electric coffeepot and filled it with water. She would surprise her dad with a hot cup of coffee as soon as he walked downstairs.

Collette searched the refrigerator and finally found the bag of coffee grounds. She flipped the bag front and back, looking for directions. They didn't give any. Collette sighed, then grabbed a spoon and added four full teaspoons. Making coffee had to be like making hot chocolate.

"Lexington Middle School, Lower Burrell Elementary, Masloff Elementary in Shaler, Murdock Elementary . . ."

Collette got out the toaster and plugged it in, then put rye and white bread next to it. She even cut the butter into little squares like they did in fancy restaurants. It looked very professional so far.

"Oliver Heights Elementary, Paynter Elementary, Proctor Middle School, Peabody High School, Reserve Elementary . . ."

Collette grabbed a chair and brought it over to the cabinet above the sink. She took down Gramma's special tiny china bowl that they always put the mint jelly in for Easter. Today was kind of a special day. Collette was sure her mother wouldn't mind if she put some grape jam in it for breakfast.

"Richland Township High School and all elementary schools, Sacred Heart Elementary and High School . . ."

"Yes!" cried Collette, holding up both hands and spinning around the kitchen. "No school!"

Mr. Murphy walked in. "Well, this is a nice surprise! Now you won't have to miss a day. How long have you been up, peanut?"

Collette hugged her father, then stepped back and straightened his tie. He looked so handsome in his gray suit.

"Just a little bit. Sit down and I'll pour you some coffee."

"Hey, I think I'm going to be spoiled," Mr. Murphy laughed. He sat down and reached for the cereal.

Collette hurried to get out the milk and juice. She poured the milk into one of the cute cream pitchers her mother kept in the china closet.

As Collette started to pour the coffee, she noticed that it wasn't very dark. In fact, it looked more like dirty river water than coffee. Her father must have noticed it, too. But he smiled up at Collette and then added two sugars and lots of cream. Collette watched as he took a tiny sip.

"Great. This sure is . . . great!"

Collette smiled. Things were going okay so far. She put in some rye bread and stood by the toaster until both pieces popped up. As she carried the plate over, with the little squares of butter arranged in an orderly circle, she could tell her father was impressed.

"You must have been up for hours getting all this ready," he said.

"Not really." Collette slid into a chair next to him. "If we got a morning paper, I would have had that right next to your coffee."

Mr. Murphy smiled and took another tiny sip of coffee. He added a little more sugar and cream and stirred it.

"Is the coffee okay, Daddy?"

"Fine. I usually try not to drink too much before I go into court. It makes me jumpy." Mr. Murphy glanced at his watch and took another bite of toast. "I'd better get going. Traffic is going to move slowly with this weather." He took out a pen and wrote some numbers down on his napkin. "Peanut, this is my office number, the courthouse number, Mom's doctor, and you know Mrs. Cessano's. Mrs. Cillo said she would try to stop by to see if you need anything."

Collette felt her heart jump beneath her thick

robe. "Why are you leaving the doctor's number? Mom is okay, isn't she?"

Her father put his arms around her. "Sure. She slept like a rock last night. But I think I should leave the number, just like I do with our other sitters."

Collette squeezed her father back. It was nice he was treating her like a real sitter. Except for the hugs, of course.

After her father left, Collette cleaned up the kitchen and waited. Any minute now the other kids would come racing downstairs and want breakfast. She retied her robe and made sure there were three cereal bowls on the table and three juice glasses. Collette walked around the table, searching for anything she may have missed. After a moment, she added a bowl of fresh fruit, then took away the salt and pepper. Finally, she took a small vase of silk flowers from the hall and put it next to the jelly bowl.

It looked wonderful.

By seven-thirty, the whole house was still quiet. Collette had already rearranged the magazines in the living room and shined the dining room table with a dish towel. She tiptoed upstairs to check on her mother, who was sound asleep. The whole house was still asleep.

Finally Collette went back down to the game room and turned on the television, listening once again to the long list of school closings. She didn't want to take a chance that Sacred Heart had secretly been reopened while she had been dusting.

"Collette!"

Collette bolted upright from the couch. "What? What?"

Stevie shook Collette's shoulder. "I'm awake and so is everyone. Mommy needs some more juice. Jeff says his bread is burning up inside the toaster and Laura is crying because her valentine box isn't fixed."

Collette tripped on her long robe as she hurried up the stairs. When had she fallen asleep? The last school closing she remembered was Lexington Run Elementary.

Collette couldn't believe her eyes. Her beautiful kitchen was in ruins. Smoke and jelly smears were everywhere. Laura was cutting out red hearts on the floor and Jeff was screaming at the toaster as if it had deliberately stolen his bread.

"See what I mean?" Stevie said softly. "I think we need Debbie."

Collette instantly felt insulted. Everything had been under control until everyone else woke up and ruined things. She readjusted her silk flower arrangement and straightened the butter dish. She carefully removed one of Stevie's little G.I. Joe men from the center of the jelly dish. "Okay now, let's just start over. Jeff, stop screaming before Mom gets out of bed. Laura, stop crying over your dumb box. . . ."

Laura looked stricken. "It's not dumb. It's my valentine box and I have to bring it in tomorrow or no one will give me any valentines. . . ." Laura rubbed both eyes with the end of her nightgown. "You're mean, Collette."

Collette stepped over Laura and unplugged the toaster so she could shake it upside down. She finally managed to remove the toast in five separate pieces.

Jeff scowled at the toast as if Collette had just grabbed them up from the bottom of the waste can.

"I'm not eating that." Jeff slid down into his seat

and crossed his arms. "I'm hungry. What's for breakfast?"

Collette drew in a deep breath and reminded herself she was the baby-sitter, not just a sister. She walked slowly to the cabinet and took out a box of Fruity Pebbles. Instead of pounding it on top of Jeff's rude head, she set it down with a quiet thump next to his bowl. "Have some cereal."

Next Collette stooped down beside Laura. She held up a red heart. It looked like a lima bean.

"This . . . this is pretty, Laura."

Laura blinked twice, releasing two fat tears. "I can't make hearts, no matter how hard I try. I'll never get any valentines."

Collette reached for the scissors. After six quick snips, the lima bean looked exactly like a small perfect heart. Laura held the heart out in front of her like Collette had just given her a beautiful jewel. She leaned over and kissed Collette twice. "Thank you, Collette. I didn't mean it when I said you were mean."

Collette hugged Laura back. "I know. I'll make you lots of hearts after breakfast, okay?"

Jeff was still staring at his cereal. "This milk tastes sour. I can't eat my cereal."

"Jeff, the milk is fine!"

Collette picked up the milk carton and pointed to the date. "Look, this is good till the twentieth. It's only the thirteenth."

"Yeah, but look at it. That milk looks peach or something."

Stevie put both hands behind his back. "I didn't do it."

"Do what?" Collette held up the milk carton. The milk did look funny. It wasn't white at all. Collette opened the lid wider and sniffed. It smelled funny, like . . . like orange juice.

Collette looked at Stevie. Stevie put both hands over his eyes.

"I didn't add orange juice. It must have been a robber guy!"

Jeff groaned and got up to dump his cereal down the sink. "You did it, Stevie. Why did you mix orange juice with the milk? Boy, are you stupid."

Stevie took a step closer to Collette. " 'Cause we didn't have too much milk and we had lots of juice, that's why."

Collette walked over to the sink and poured the milk down the drain. When she went to the refrigerator, she realized she had just dumped the last of the milk down the sink.

"Oh, Stevie." Collette sighed. "We don't have any milk now."

Laura handed Collette her only perfect heart. "Here, Collette, you can hold this."

Collette frowned as she looked around the cluttered kitchen. The clock on the stove read eight-fifteen. Her father wouldn't be home until six-thirty. Ten hours! Six-thirty seemed like forever.

"Maybe we can borrow some milk from Marsha," suggested Jeff. "They don't have Stevies over there ruining their milk."

Collette glanced at the phone, wondering if Marsha was even up yet. She probably was. Sitting at the breakfast table in her white monogrammed robe, eating homemade biscuits.

"Collette!"

Collette spun around as she heard her mother's voice from upstairs. She had forgotten all about her mother's juice.

"Hey, everyone act like you're having breakfast," Collette instructed. "Mom isn't supposed to get out of bed all day so we have to act like everything is fine."

Jeff held up two burned squares of toast. "Yeah, well, everything isn't fine . . . I'm hungry!"

"I have to have my valentine box ready for tomorrow!" wailed Laura. "My teacher *said*."

Stevie leaned against Collette's leg. "I was only trying to help. I didn't mean to ruin stuff. Nobody likes me."

Collette patted Stevie on the head. "Everyone likes you, Stevie."

If everyone could just pretend things were fine, then they would be. Outside the wind howled.

"Wow, that sounds like the witch lady looking for some dogs to eat," Jeff said in a low spooky voice. "She's outside looking."

Stevie buried his face in Collette's robe. Laura picked up the scissors and stared out the window.

"Jeff, don't tease!" Collette said automatically. She took the juice and headed upstairs. Stevie was still attached to her leg, so she moved slowly. By the time she reached the top step, she was puffing for breath as though she had just climbed the Alps.

Collette glanced at the clock in the hall. She was completely exhausted and it was still only eight twenty-five in the morning! At the rate she was going, she wouldn't be able to last until lunch.

Chapter Eleven

An hour later Collette carried in the small black-and-white television set for her mother.

"Collette, don't worry about me," Mrs. Murphy laughed. She scooted up in bed and reached for Collette's hand. "Save all your strength for the troops downstairs. It's too cold to let them play outside, so I'm sure you're going to need all the energy you can muster."

Collette hoped her laugh sounded carefree enough. She didn't want her mother to have to worry about a thing. All she was supposed to do was stay in bed and let the baby have lots of rest.

"So what does all this bed rest do for the baby, anyway?" asked Collette. Her mother was almost three months pregnant so the baby couldn't be that big.

Mrs. Murphy sighed. "Well, if I'm going to have a miscarriage, it usually occurs during the first three months."

"What?" Collette could barely breathe for a second. Was her mother telling her that this had happened before?

Mrs. Murphy looked up, her faced flushed red instantly. "Oh, honey, I'm sorry. Of course you didn't know."

Collette sat down next to her mother. "You mean, you already *had* one miscarriage? When? How come I can't remember it?"

"I had one miscarriage before you were born, and one between Jeff and Laura. I was barely three months with each but it was still very sad."

Collette felt her arms prickle cold with the shocking news. News that nobody had ever bothered telling her. "So there really should be six kids?"

Her mother brushed back Collette's hair. "If a baby isn't strong enough . . ."

"I know." Collette sighed. "Daddy already told me. Gosh, Mom, this is serious then. I mean, if you had those other miscarriages, you could do it again."

Mrs. Murphy gave Collette's hair a gentle tug. "But I had four healthy, big babies. I like to think of that and realize I can do *that* again."

Collette leaned against her mother. "I know, but listen, Mom. You have to promise me that you will let me do everything, okay? We can't take any chances with this baby."

Mother laughed. "Aye, aye, Captain. But I think you should call Sarah or Marsha to come over and help, so you won't be outnumbered. Your day can get pretty long with three children needing five hundred things."

Collette stood up and shrugged. "I can handle it. Daddy already told me I was doing a great job." Collette smiled. "We'll be busy today. Jeff wants cookies and Laura is still having a super fit because her valentine box still looks exactly like a shoe box."

"Good luck. I'm here if you need me."

Collette turned on the television and walked briskly out of her mother's room. "Relax, Mom." As long as she continued to do a perfect job, there would be no reason to worry.

She raced downstairs and made everyone toast with lots of grape jam. Even Jeff said thank you.

"Can we start my cookies soon?" asked Jeff. "We can't forget about them, Collette. My teacher said."

Laura plunked down her scissors. "Well, my teacher said that we have to make this valentine box. All my glue marks are showing right through my hearts. My hearts look wet!"

Jeff leaned over and studied the lumpy-looking box. "That's 'cause you have about five pounds of glue under each heart, Laura. You don't shovel it on, you just use a little."

Collette wiped off her hands and shooed everyone out of the kitchen. "I'll help you all once I get this junk cleaned up. Go downstairs and watch cartoons or something."

She smiled as she sank both hands deep into the warm soapy water. She had made it through breakfast and two almost-fights and she hadn't had to bother her mother once.

After the kitchen was clean again, Collette called Marsha. "Marsha, hi . . . I didn't wake you up, did I?" Collette twisted around to glance at the clock. It was exactly ten o'clock in the morning.

"Listen, Marsha, I was wondering if I could borrow a few things."

"Sure," Marsha replied between yawns. "My mom just left but she won't care. What do you need?"

Collette picked up her list from the kitchen table. "Well, four eggs, a quart of milk, flour, sugar, three teaspoons of vanilla and . . . and two pieces of red construction paper."

"What?" Marsha sounded wide awake now. "What on earth are you guys making over there?"

Collette laughed. "Everything. Jeff needs cookies for tomorrow, Stevie wants to make Debbie a fifty-pound sugar cookie, and Laura just dumped glue over our last sheet of red construction paper."

Marsha was quiet for a minute. "Holy cow. Your mom must be feeling *a lot* better."

"No. I mean, she is, but she still can't get out of bed till Monday." Collette wrapped the phone cord around her fingers. She didn't want to tell anyone about the miscarriages. It was probably supposed to be private, family stuff, anyway. And her mother *was* feeling better and she wasn't throwing up anymore. Only four more days of keeping fingers crossed. By Monday Collette was sure the baby would be theirs to keep.

"Collette, my mom and I didn't mean anything bad about . . . well, I mean, we don't *really* think your mom is too old or anything." Marsha was quiet for a second. "I hope she feels better. My mom hopes so, too. She made lots of phone calls last night, trying to cancel this card party today. She really wanted to help baby-sit, but all these old people are being bused in from a nursing home to play bridge and they would be really disappointed. Gosh, our family feels kind of crummy for saying you guys already *had* too many kids. I mean, my mom even said she would love to send dinner over Friday night, and — "

"Marsha," Collette broke in. "We're fine over here. And . . . well, thanks for saying all that about the baby. I . . . we're all real happy about the baby now, too. It will be fun to have a little baby in the family."

"I know. I wish my mom would get pregnant. I told my parents I would watch the baby for free." Marsha laughed. "So anyway, who did your dad finally get to baby-sit?"

Collette bit her lip so she wouldn't laugh out loud. "Me."

"What?" Collette knew Marsha's eyes were probably ready to bug out of her head. "You mean *just you?*"

"Sure." Collette glanced around the spotless kitchen. "Things are going great. My mom is having some hot coffee that I made all by myself, and some toast. I was just about to bake some sugar cookies for Jeff. That's why I need all that flour and stuff. Who knows, if I get bored I might just throw in a couple of loads of laundry."

"Since when did you do laundry?" hooted Marsha. "Last time I was over there, you didn't even know how to throw it down the laundry chute."

"How hard can laundry be?" Collette pictured her mother downstairs, dipping the measuring cup inside the detergent, twisting a few dials, choosing hot or cold water. Playing some video games seemed a lot trickier.

"I'm going to get dressed and be right over. Promise me you won't start anything until I get there. I want to see Laura's valentine box and I've got to see you trying to be in charge of those wild brothers of yours. Okay?"

"Okay!"

After Collette hung up, she walked through the

house fluffing pillows, and checking to make sure all the living room windows were locked tight against the bitter wind. Collette sank into the rocking chair and smiled. She could hear Stevie laughing upstairs. So far things were working out perfectly. Collette started rocking. She knew wishes didn't *always* come true, and you didn't *automatically* get whatever you prayed for. But wishes did come true sometimes, and her mother always said that God heard every prayer. So maybe if Collette worked hard this whole day to make sure everyone was happy and taken care of, then God would zap the little baby with extra strength so he could be born in six months. With each rock, Collette counted off another month . . . March, April, May and June, July, August. . . . Collette grinned, picturing the baby in a tiny little bathing suit at the end of August. That would be so cute. . . .

"Collette!" Jeff raced into the room and skidded right into the arm of the rocking chair. "Get upstairs fast!" Collette bolted up so quickly, the rocker banged hard against the wall. "Oh, gosh, Mom isn't sick is she?"

"No, but Laura locked herself in the bathroom."

Collette groaned as she hurried up the stairs.

Holy cow, why would Laura lock that door when their dad had told her a thousand times the door was too old to lock?

"Collette!" her mother called. "What is going on out there? What's all the yelling about?"

Collette skidded to a stop outside her mother's room, brushing back her hair and trying to steady her breathing. Jeff followed her in.

"Well, hi, Mom . . . how are you feeling? Do you want another cup of coffee?"

Collette saw her mother's worried expression. "No thanks. Why is Laura screaming?"

Collette raised an eyebrow, as if she really hadn't heard Laura's cries for help. Laura would probably start crying harder when Collette informed her there *wasn't* a key to the bathroom. She didn't have the slightest idea how to get Laura out. The last time Stevie locked himself inside, Daddy had to call a locksmith and hand him a check for sixty-five dollars.

"Oh . . . that . . . well, I think Laura accidentally locked herself in the bathroom." Collette said it quickly and tried to end with a smile. The last thing she wanted was to have her mother hop out of bed and try to take the heavy bathroom door

86

off. "I was just about to go check on her."

Mrs. Murphy pushed back the quilt and sighed. "*Why* did she lock the door? Tell Laura I'll be right there."

Jeff and Collette both reached out and gently pushed their mother back against the pillows. "No way!"

"Dad would be so mad," warned Jeff. "He said you were to stay in bed all day. No matter what."

"Besides," Collette spoke up. "I'm the baby-sitter and I'm in charge. You stay in bed and Jeff and I will get Laura out of the bathroom."

Mrs. Murphy pulled the quilt back up, but she still looked worried. "Well, please hurry up and get her out."

Another high-pitched squeal from Laura was followed by Stevie bolting into the room. He dove across his mother's bed and hid his head under the bedspread.

"It was *only* a joke," he shouted. "Jeff would have laughed."

Collette heard Laura scream again. She pulled the bedspread back and rolled Stevie over so he had to look her right in the eye. "What did you do *now*, Stevie?"

"I was only trying to make Laura laugh."

"What did you *do*, Stevie?" Mrs. Murphy asked. Nobody was smiling now.

"I just tolded Laura that a big black spider lives in the toilet and he was coming up to bite her!"

"Stevie!" cried Collette. She turned and ran down the hall. "Laura, here I come. Stevie was only kidding about the big spider."

Collette jiggled the bathroom's glass doorknob. She pressed hard against the door with her hip.

"Collette, is she out yet?" called Mrs. Murphy from her bedroom.

"Almost!" Collette cringed for lying, but she would burst into tears if her mother got out of bed.

Stevie bent down and put his eye against the crack of the door. "Laura, it's not a *real big* spider! He's just little with no hair on his legs, and . . ."

As Laura started to scream again, Collette grabbed Stevie up by the arm. "Go call Marsha and tell her Laura is locked in the bathroom. Ask her if she can come over right away to help."

Stevie nodded. "But I don't know her phone number."

Collette felt like screaming herself. "It's 555-24 — oh, never mind. Laura, I'll be right back!"

"NO, Collette. Don't leave me," wailed Laura. "Hold my fingers!"

"What?"

Collette looked down and saw Laura's two little fingers peeking out from beneath the bathroom door.

"I want Mommy!" sobbed Laura.

Collette stooped down and put the tips of her fingers against Laura's. She could tell Laura was about to start screaming again.

"Wait, Laura." Collette looked up at Stevie. "Go get your coat on and run across the street and get Marsha, Stevie. Tell her to hurry up, okay?"

Stevie nodded. He held his hands up in prayer. "I'll be real good the rest of the day, okay, Collette? Don't tell Daddy about the spider."

"*I'll* tell him!" shouted Laura from behind the door. "This is all your fault, Stevie. I only locked myself in this bathroom because you chased me with your stinky socks. Daddy is going to be real mad!"

Stevie's eyes flew open.

Collette reached out and patted Stevie's leg. "But if you go get Marsha, then we can tell Daddy how much you helped."

Stevie turned. "Let's tell Daddy the part about me helping first, and *then* the spider part, okay?" Stevie raced down the stairs. Collette wiggled her fingers against Laura's and leaned her head against the door.

"Collette, I'm hungry. What if I have to eat soap?"

Collette swallowed a groan. "Laura, you just finished breakfast. Don't worry. You will be out before you get hungry."

"But I didn't *eat* my breakfast because Stevie ruined the milk. You better tell Daddy how bad Stevie is. I bet Stevie tries to bite our new baby. Maybe we should send Stevie to a far, faraway camp till next summer. Let's tell Daddy that, too, okay?"

Collette nodded. It was still morning and she already had a list of things to tell her father. Too bad she could never show the list to him. If he read it, he would realize he had made a mistake hiring Collette as a sitter.

Collette drew in a deep breath and gave Laura's fingertip a squeeze. No matter what, this day was going to stay perfect. It had to.

"Collette . . . is Laura okay?" Mrs. Murphy called.

"Yes!" To make sure Laura didn't start screaming her head off, Collette started telling funny stories. She was finished with "The Three Pigs" and just about to start "Jack and the Beanstalk," when Marsha came clomping upstairs, still in her boots. When she reached the landing, she yanked off her hat and swallowed three times before she could speak.

"Collette, come outside *right away!*"

Collette frowned at the snow puddles forming around Marsha's boots. Another mess she was going to have to clean up! Couldn't Marsha see she was in the middle of a crisis?

"Marsha, you're dripping all over," said Jeff, moving away.

"Hurry!" urged Marsha, bending down and grabbing Collette under the armpits with two ice cold mittens.

"Marsha, what are you doing? I can't leave now!"

Marsha waved her ski cap, and lowered her voice. "Well, you'd *better* come right now! Stevie said my brass doorknob looked just like a huge scoop of gold ice cream, and I laughed, said it was, and before I knew it, your stupid little brother bent down and licked it. Stevie *licked our doorknob* and his tongue is like . . . frozen to it!"

Collette stood up so quickly, she felt dizzy. "How stuck is he?"

Marsha rolled her eyes. "Well, so stuck that his tongue is stretched out about ten or twenty inches!" Marsha pulled on Collette's arm. "Come on!"

"Cool," cried Jeff.

"Wait, Collette!" cried Laura. "Get me out quick so I can go see! I've never seen a glued-down tongue before."

"Jeff, you stay with Laura. I'll be right back."

Collette followed Marsha down the stairs, and jumped into her boots and coat. Poor Stevie. He had to be scared to death. The baby-sitter would have to help. Collette was halfway down the driveway when she skidded to a sudden stop. Wait a minute, *she* was the baby-sitter. A baby-sitter who didn't have a clue in the world about unsticking a stuck tongue.

Chapter Twelve

As soon as Collette saw Stevie, the huge tears streaming down his face, and his small pink tongue attached to Marsha's huge brass doorknob, she wished a lady from the baby-sitting agency was following right behind her.

Collette kept patting Stevie on the back until she remembered he wasn't choking. It was Marsha's idea to pour warm water over Stevie's tongue. "Get ready to grab him away as soon as the water hits," shouted Marsha. Collette had never seen Marsha so worried. Her hand shook as she poured the gigantic bucket of water over Stevie's face.

Collette pulled Stevie away and then wiped his

mouth off fast with her scarf. She didn't want his whole face freezing to Marsha's front door.

"Good work, Marsha," said Collette. She spun Stevie around and hugged him. Stevie was shaking so hard his teeth were chattering. His eyes crossed as he tried to examine his tongue.

"Come on. We better get Stevie home before he turns into an ice sculpture. Marsha, grab the flour and construction paper and come back over." Collette turned and smiled at Marsha as she steered Stevie across the snow. "Thanks for unsticking Stevie. Where did you ever learn that?"

Marsha took a small bow. "The lock to my dad's car was frozen last night when we came out of Wendy's. He dumped his hot coffee on the lock."

"My tongue is broken," Stevie cried. "I want Mommy to put a bandage on it."

Collette shook her head. "No, we *can't* tell Mom, Stevie. It would only make her worry. Besides, I don't think they make bandages for tongues. Let's go and tell Jeff and Laura you're okay . . ."

Collette twisted around to stare at her house. Laura! "Come on, guys. We still have to get Laura out of the bathroom."

"Wait, I'll bring a key!" announced Marsha. She raced back into her house and came running out with a large brown bag. "Come on, follow me."

"Marsha is a good fixer," announced Stevie. "She should be our baby-sitter. You want to baby-sit me, Marsha?"

Collette felt insulted as she hurried to catch up with Marsha. Stevie was forgetting how well Collette had taken care of them until his tongue got glued to the doorknob. And it certainly wasn't her fault that Laura locked herself in the bathroom.

The house was surprisingly quiet. In fact, the house was a little *too* quiet. Collette hurried upstairs after Marsha, too worried about Laura to think about the snowy mess they were tracking in.

Jeff was still sitting outside the bathroom door, wearing his New York Mets hat and sliding baseball cards under the crack. "Now this guy, Dwight Gooden, is a pitcher for the Mets. He was so good last season that this card is probably already worth a lot. Maybe three dollars . . ."

"I'll give you all my baseball cards if you get me out, Jeff. . . . Show me another Pirate card," Laura said from behind the door. "Do you have Doug Drabek?"

"We're back," announced Marsha. She set down her bag and pulled out the flour, sugar, construction paper, and eggs. Finally Marsha pulled out a long, thin metal rod. "Here it is. Okay, Jeff, step aside. This should work."

"Marsha is *real* smart," announced Stevie. "She unsticked my tongue."

Jeff stood up and stared into Stevie's open mouth. "Let me see. Did any of it get ripped off?"

"Wait, Stevie. Let me see, too!" cried Laura. "Stevie, stick your tongue through the crack."

"Wait a sec," ordered Marsha. "Everyone stand back. I need room." Marsha jabbed the long thin rod into the keyhole.

"Holy cow. What is that?" asked Collette. "Is it some sort of weapon?"

Marsha turned, smiling across her shoulder. "No . . . a knitting needle. My little cousin is always getting stuck in their bathroom. My uncle uses a long nail, but this should work." Marsha bit her lip as she jiggled and poked the needle around the keyhole. Finally a little popping sound was heard and she flung the door open. "Ta daaa!"

Laura came rushing out, and wrapped her arms around Marsha's waist. "Thank you. You saved me, Marsha. Now I won't have to eat soap."

Collette was so glad that Laura was finally out, she didn't even bother to yell at her about locking the door. She also pretended not to see when Stevie accidentally stepped on one of the eggs. "Thanks, Marsha. Boy, you should sign up with a baby-sitting agency. Okay, guys, now . . . Stevie, get some tissue and clean up the egg mess. Then let's all go downstairs and relax, okay?"

"Maybe we should start making those cookies," suggested Jeff. He frowned at Stevie. "After Stevie borrows another egg."

"And we have to finish making my valentine box," added Laura. "I have to have it by tomorrow. My teacher said."

Stevie's eyes crossed again as he stuck out his tongue and tried to study it. "My tongue hurts too much to clean up that dumb egg. Call Daddy and tell him to come home."

Collette shook her head. "Daddy's in court. The judge gets mad if you interrupt. Listen, Stevie, I'll help you clean up the egg. Then I'll get you some ginger ale for your sore tongue and you can help with the cookies, okay?"

"Laura?" Mrs. Murphy was calling from her bedroom. "Are you finally out, honey?"

Laura smiled and raced into her mother's room. "Marsha stuck a knife in the door and saved me."

Mrs. Murphy looked a little alarmed. "A knife?"

Marsha held up the blue knitting needle. "It's a knitting needle."

"Well, thank you, Marsha." Mrs. Murphy smiled. "I guess we'd better buy some knitting needles in case this happens again."

Stevie peered inside Marsha's bag. "Can I play with one? It would make a cool flagpole for my G.I. Joe men." He reached in and pulled out a handful of pale green yarn. "Oh, man, you have nice junk in here. Can I have some of this to tie up Jeff?"

Marsha snatched back the yarn. "No, don't get in there, Stevie. It's . . ."

Collette picked up the ball of yarn that had fallen and handed it back to Marsha. "What's your mom making?"

Marsha's face blushed pink, then grew to a rosy

red. "I'm knitting something . . . I really don't know how to do it yet."

Stevie reached in and pulled out a two-inch square. "This is a nice little stamp, Marsha. Are you going to knit an envelope, too?"

Collette watched as Marsha's face grew redder and redder. She looked like a lobster, fresh from the pot. Why was she so upset after she'd been a hero?

Mrs. Murphy reached out and pulled Marsha closer to the bed. "Stevie wasn't trying to hurt your feelings, Marsha. It looks very nice so far."

"It could be a good blanket for my G.I. Joe men," added Stevie.

Marsha sighed. "Well, I . . . it's going to be . . . be a blanket for your new baby . . ." Marsha glanced up at Mrs. Murphy. "I sure am sorry you have to stay in bed, Mrs. Murphy. I said a prayer last night just for your baby."

Mrs. Murphy reached over and hugged Marsha. "Thanks, Marsha. I hope I'll be out of bed soon. Maybe you can teach me how to knit, too. I could make a few squares and sew them together with yours."

Collette nodded along with Marsha. That

sounded like a great plan. Maybe they could all make a square out of something, like her old quilt, or Stevie's faded football shirt he finally outgrew. The baby would love to be covered up by all their love.

Marsha stood up and pushed everything back in her bag. "Sure, I could teach you. I mean, I don't know too much, but . . ."

Stevie grinned up at Marsha. "But you know a lot about stuck tongues, right?"

Mrs. Murphy leaned forward. "What?"

Collette broke in front of Stevie and fluffed up her mother's pillow. She didn't want her mom to hear about the frozen tongue just yet. With any luck, each crisis would be separated by two-hour breaks.

"Mom, you just relax. We are going downstairs to start the cookies."

Collette was glad to see her mother smile.

"Gosh, I think I might just get up and wash my hair." Mrs. Murphy ran her fingers through her thick dark hair and made a face. "It feels so dirty."

"No, Mom," Jeff said quickly. "Dad said you weren't allowed out of bed except to go to the bathroom. Don't wash anything."

Mrs. Murphy grinned. "Jeff, relax. It would only take me five minutes."

"Unless you got locked in the bathroom," reminded Laura. "It takes longer then."

Collette sighed. "Stay in bed, Mom. I don't think I could take another emergency right now." She put her hand on Stevie's shoulder. "Understand, Stevie."

Stevie looked up innocently. "I'm the goodest one here."

Collette herded everyone out and started to close her mother's door. "You can wash your hair tomorrow."

Jeff pushed the door open and tossed his mother his baseball cap. "Here, wear this. No one can tell how awful your hair looks!"

"Jeff!" Collette laughed. "Mom, I'm turning off the television and the lights so you can get some sleep."

"Good idea," agreed Mrs. Murphy. "A nap sounds great!"

Marsha grabbed Collette's arm as they all started down the stairs.

"Too bad your mom doesn't have that old-fashioned shampoo my gram used when she was in the hospital," said Marsha. "It was cool. You dump this white powder on dirty hair and it soaks up all the grease. You brush it out and it looks great!"

Collette laughed. "Marsha, you have an answer for everything today!"

"Yes, and I will send you a bill for my consultations."

Stevie slipped his hand in Marsha's. "I'll be your big helper, okay?"

"Thanks, buddy."

Collette took a step back, a tiny bit jealous that Stevie was acting like *Marsha* was his big sister, not her. The jealousy only flickered for a second.

It was great that Stevie liked Marsha a lot. Because once the new baby came, Collette would be awfully busy helping her mom take care of it. Besides, the day was going better, so no one should be unhappy about anything. Everyone was talking and laughing now. Nobody was in a bad mood. Her mother might drift off to sleep, and the snow outside was falling again in fat silent flakes.

The grandfather clock down in the living room started to chime. . . . nine, ten, eleven, twelve. Collette smiled. Her first whole day of baby-sitting was exactly half over and things were still perfect.

Collette was just putting down the supplies on the kitchen table when the lights started to flicker. Next the radio squawked and faded and the microwave clock started to flash. Then everything went dark and still.

Chapter Thirteen

"Collette! The lights went out!" cried Laura. She ran to the window. "Maybe it's too cold for the electricity to work."

Collette slumped into the chair. Oh, brother! Sometimes the electricity went off and *stayed off* for hours. It would get darker and darker and . . .

"Now we can't make my cookies," complained Jeff. "Oh, man. Is there a no-oven cookie recipe? I don't even care what they taste like. Just so they *look* like a cookie."

Marsha and Collette exchanged puzzled looks. They were both so new to cooking, they weren't sure. Maybe . . .

104

Jeff opened the cabinets. "How about peanut butter and jelly rolled in sugar and . . ."

"And a cherry on top!" sang out Laura.

Collette flicked the light switch on and off while Marsha peered out the window. "I wonder if the whole block is out of electricity."

"I am so mad," declared Stevie. "Now I can't watch that soap show. Debbie tolded me that Brad was going to do something bad by Friday." Stevie sniffed. "Now I'm going to miss all that good fighting stuff."

Collette rolled her eyes. Getting *Lives of Lies* out of their house was the only plus of being without lights, heat . . .

Heat! The furnace was electric! What were they going to do when the temperature dropped to minus ten degrees inside her own kitchen? Oh, gosh, what would really, really cold temperatures do to her mother and the baby? What if the baby got weaker and weaker when her mom's body temperature dropped?

"Jeff, do we have any firewood left?" asked Collette. She remembered her dad had ordered a whole stack of it for Thanksgiving. If they had lots of wood, at least her mother could sit on the couch in front of a nice warm fire.

"I'll go check," said Jeff. "Laura, come and help me carry up some logs from the workroom."

"Marsha, do you know how to open the chimney flue vent and start a fire?" asked Collette. She had watched her father start them lots of times, but even *he* had a hard time jiggling the old chain. If you didn't do it right, the whole house could fill with smoke. Her mother shouldn't breathe in smoke while she was pregnant.

Marsha, not looking the least bit worried, just shrugged.

Collette turned and raced out of the kitchen, taking the stairs two at a time. She would have to break the news gently to her mother, since she didn't want her to get upset. If her mother went slowly down the stairs, she would be all right. Maybe she could rest after every step, and Jeff and Collette could each hold an arm.

Once outside her mother's door, Collette shook back her hair and drew in a deep breath. She would use an old trick of her mother's and pretend that the whole business of having no electricity was going to be one, big *fun* adventure. They could sit around the fire, telling stories and eating cold cheese sandwiches till Daddy came home. Maybe by that time all the lights and radio would flash on, filling the house with noise and heat.

Collette put her hand on the doorknob, feeling more confident by the second. Her mother was already feeling better, so a trip downstairs wouldn't be all *that* terrible and —

"Stevie!"

Collette's words seemed to freeze Stevie into stone. He stood atop Mrs. Murphy's bed, holding a can of baby powder. White powder drifted down on Mrs. Murphy's head as she slept.

"Stevie Murphy! What in the world are you doing?" hissed Collette.

Stevie dropped the can of baby powder and put both hands behind his back. "It was going to be a surprise . . ."

Mrs. Murphy's eyes flew open and she struggled to sit up as a white pile of powder avalanched down the front of her face. "What is — " Mrs. Murphy sputtered and rubbed both eyes. "What *is* this stuff? What is going on?"

Collette rushed forward and brushed a handful of powder from the top of her mother's head. "Stevie was trying to . . ."

Stevie crumbled on top of the bed and started to cry. "I was only trying to get rid of your grease . . . Marsha said her grandma liked hair powder and . . ." He flopped back against the pillows and sniffed loudly. "I don't know how I get in all this trouble. Don't tell Daddy."

Collette started to smile. It really was kind of funny. Her mother looked like an old lady.

"What is so funny? Why did he dump a can of baby powder on me?" Mrs. Murphy looked over at Collette and frowned. "Where were you, Collette?"

Collette felt as if her mother had just slapped her. Where had she been? She had been downstairs, trying to organize a fire squad so icicles wouldn't start forming. Surely her mother didn't think she had been downstairs playing crazy eights with Marsha!

"I was downstairs. Stevie wasn't trying to be bad. You see, Marsha mentioned that dry shampoo stuff they use in hospitals and . . ." Collette sat down on the bed next to her mother and sighed. "He was just trying to help."

Stevie lifted his head and stared at Collette. "Am I in trouble?"

Mrs. Murphy shook her head, white powder plopping down on her cheeks. She smiled. "I think I'm beginning to understand." She patted Stevie's hand. "Thanks, honey. Sorry I yelled."

Stevie smiled. "I think you have to comb your hair and then it works. You look kind of dusty now."

Collette handed her mother a brush. "You'd better brush it before you get out of bed. Jeff and I can help you downstairs. You'll be warmer there."

Mrs. Murphy looked even more confused.

Collette drew in a deep breath, hoping her mother wouldn't be upset. "The electricity went off about five minutes ago. We should start a fire so you and the baby won't catch cold."

Collette saw the alarm register in her mother's eyes. Then she smiled and started brushing her long dark hair briskly. "Oh, well . . . usually that happens at least once during the winter. Sometimes it comes right back on."

Collette nodded. *Sometimes* the electricity would go right back on, but not while Collette Murphy was in charge of the house. With the way the day had been going, the electricity would still be off when her dad got home from work. Mr.

Murphy would walk into a dark, cold house and have to eat saltine crackers for dinner and chip ice off his glass of milk.

Collette straightened her back and smiled down at her mother. Staying in a good mood, no matter what, was rule number one in baby-sitting perfectly. Collette could do that. She had to. There was much too much at stake to quit now.

Chapter Fourteen

"Isn't this fun?" Collette laughed as she heard her mother's voice coming out of her own mouth. But actually, with the fire finally going and the cereal bowls filled with peanuts, cheese cubes, and potato chips, it *was* a lot of fun.

Collette was glad to see her mother's cheeks looking so healthy and pink in the light of the fire. Stevie had covered her with his old quilt and three beach towels. Laura had moved her valentine box next to the couch so her mother could watch her color rainbows on each side. "I am really amazed. You kids built a great fire."

Collette and Marsha grinned at each other. It had taken five minutes to get the vent open, but arranging the logs into a teepee shape and stuffing rolled-up paper in the middle had been fun. Marsha's mother had called just after they had lit the first match to say that the electricity was out in Harmarville, too. As soon as she helped pack up the elderly visitors, Mrs. Cessano wanted to stay and help clean up. With traffic, she might not be home until five-thirty. Collette felt very important as she talked to Mrs. Cessano. Kind of baby-sitter to adult. She told Marsha's mother that Marsha had been no problem and she was welcome to stay as long as necessary. Mrs. Cessano had laughed and promised to bring home lots of the tiny decorated cakes that had been left over from the interrupted luncheon.

Laura reached up and wrapped her thin arm around her mother's neck. "You look pretty with white hair. Stevie turned you into a good fairy."

Everyone started laughing. Stevie's eyes were huge until he finally smiled himself.

"I don't think any oil will get near my head for *at least* a month," laughed Mrs. Murphy. "I'll have to tell Daddy all about my beauty salon treatment next time he calls to check in."

Collette glanced up at the clock; it was almost

four o'clock. Her dad would be calling to check in again any minute. So far, Collette or her mother had given him good reports. Collette crossed her fingers. She wanted the reports to stay that way. So far her father thought Collette was doing a perfect job with everyone. A lot had happened so far, but nothing too terrible. Nothing so terrible that she had to worry her dad about it during a court case. Collette reached for another cheese cube, then leaned back against the couch to watch the fire. Inside her head, she had a mental checklist going. Sometimes she had gotten *too* worried about things, and other times she had *forgotten* to worry. She *did* get mad about the messy kitchen, since she had worked so hard to fix it fancy. But she had been much better about Laura in the bathroom and Stevie's tongue being stuck to the cold doorknob. And she finally convinced her mother to laugh about the baby powder. Collette looked over at Stevie as he played with his little G.I. Joe men in her mother's large green plant. Men hung from thick stems, and stood head first in the dirt. Having another little baby just like Stevie would be nice. Nobody could think the way Stevie did. And Stevie wasn't going to stay five forever. Soon he would grow up and start acting normal and not so . . . so Stevie.

Collette started to shiver, as if the window had just blown open and covered her with fresh snow. She hoped she was doing a good job baby-sitting. She wanted her mother and everyone to know that she was going to be a big help. It was so strange to even imagine a time when the thought of the new baby felt wrong. Now everyone wanted the baby, especially Collette. That had to count for something. Collette sighed, knowing things didn't always work that way. Even though everyone wanted the baby *now* and her mother was being so careful about staying off her feet, it didn't mean that the baby wouldn't go back to heaven. Only God knew what was really going to happen. That scared Collette a little. It scared her a lot. It was like climbing very carefully up the steep metal steps of the tallest slide on the playground, then slowly lowering yourself on the top and giving a push off. Everything was planned until you let go.

"Pass the peanuts," called out Jeff.

Collette handed the bowl to Marsha who handed them to Jeff. Mrs. Murphy reached out and took a quick handful and everyone laughed. "Mind if I take a shortcut?"

"What's so funny?" asked Stevie. He poked his head up from behind the chair.

"Mommy's acting like a kid," explained Laura.

Just then, as if a movie director had been sitting in a canvas chair with a clipboard and megaphone, the lights went on. The radio blasted out from the kitchen, full force, and they all laughed and covered their ears.

Laura scrambled up and ran into the kitchen. The clock in the corner started to chime. Collette closed her eyes and counted each gong . . . "two, three, four, . . ."

Mrs. Murphy patted her stomach and grinned. "Four little Murphys and one more."

Collette caught her mother's eye and they both smiled, as if only the two of them caught the private joke.

"Let's start the cookies before the electricity goes off again," cried Jeff, racing back into the kitchen. "Come on, Collette."

Mrs. Murphy gathered up her towels and quilt and stretched. "I'll get back to bed and take a nap. Call me if you need any help."

Collette made sure the screen was tightly drawn in front of the fire before she walked back toward the kitchen. The bright lights in the hall and kitchen seemed to congratulate her that she had made it through a rough day. The worst was over, she knew it. Only two more hours until her dad pulled in the driveway to take over. A sitter had already been arranged with the agency for tomorrow.

Collette smiled so wide, Marsha nudged her with her elbow. "What's so funny?"

Collette just shrugged, too happy to speak. Being in charge was a snap, once you got the hang of it. She had almost convinced herself of this when she heard Jeff's screams.

Chapter Fifteen

"Bugs!" shouted Jeff, backing away from the kitchen table. "Disgusting bugs! The whole bag of flour is filled with them."

Laura tiptoed up and peeked inside. "I can't see them, Jeff. They must be hiding."

Jeff walked back and poured some of the flour into a bowl. "Look, those little brown, curled-up things. Man, we can't use this. How old is this flour, Marsha?"

Marsha's face grew pink. "I don't know. I just took it from the pantry."

Collette peered into the bowl. Tiny brown bugs were scattered around the flour like cinnamon. "Maybe they're dead. I don't see them moving."

Jeff rolled his eyes and groaned. "So what? You can't make cookies with dead bugs inside them. I'd be thrown out of the fourth grade."

Collette dumped the flour into the trash. Her mother never baked so she didn't even bother looking for flour. The only thing they had that even *looked like* flour was pancake mix. Maybe that would work.

Collette stood on her tiptoes and reached for the bright red box of pancake mix. Her mother had engulfed it in a huge plastic bag with a green twisty-tie on top. A bug would have to be a Houdini to find a way inside.

"We can use this. Let's start over. Okay, how many eggs do we have left?"

Laura's head snapped up like someone had reins attached. "Stevie broke one and . . ." Laura blinked fast. "I only cracked up one a little."

"What?" Jeff slid into a chair and covered his eyes. "I'll never end up with cookies. I'm not going to school tomorrow. That's it. I quit."

"Where is the cracked-up one, Laura?" Collette tried to keep her voice light. Jeff was already upset enough for everyone.

Laura pointed to the window. Her lower lip was quivering.

"You threw it out the window?" Collette sighed.

"No, it's on the back porch. I thought maybe the cold air would freeze up the crack."

Marsha shook her head. "What if a dog licked it?"

Stevie giggled and Jeff groaned more deeply.

"Well, we don't need *that* egg. We still have two eggs." Collette got a small checked cookbook from the drawer. "Lots of people like less egg. It's less cholesterol and . . ." Collette's finger traced halfway down the page. "How about sugar cookies?"

"Red ones!" added Laura. "To match my valentines!"

Marsha opened the pantry. "Does your mom have food coloring?"

Collette nodded, glad her mother had at least one ingredient. Her mother didn't like to bake, but she loved to dye Easter eggs.

In less than an hour, the cookies were in small pink mounds on a round pizza pan.

"Are you sure your mother doesn't have a cookie

sheet?" asked Marsha. She looked down at the pizza tin and frowned.

"Marsha, it's no *big deal*," reminded Collette. "I mean, do you think this dough realizes it's not on a real, genuine cookie sheet?"

Laura nodded. "Yeah. We had a cookie sheet once but we built a clay house on it and left it outside in the sandbox."

Jeff started to smile. He had cheered up once the cookies started to look more like cookies. "Hey, let's just get them baked. I just don't want my name to go up on the blackboard for forgetting. My teacher will be so mad."

Laura let out a yelp. "We forgot all day about my valentine box! My teacher will be mad, too."

Collette opened the oven door and popped in the cookies. Making the valentine box was the absolute last thing on her list. Once that was finished, her dad would be home. He had finally called and promised to bring home a large pizza with extra cheese, pepperoni, and sausage.

"Okay, let's get the red paper, Laura." Collette tossed Marsha a sponge and they both started to clean off the table. Laura brought in her large box. It still looked kind of plain. There were a lot of glue clumps and tiny hearts that looked like jelly beans.

Marsha tossed her sponge into the sink and studied the box. "Okay now, Laura, I think you need something kind of snazzy. Do you have any red feathers?"

Laura looked over at Collette. Collette shook her head.

"How about some glitter?" Marsha looked around the kitchen. "Or some tiny heart candy? You know, with all those silly 'Kiss Me' sayings on them."

Laura frowned. "Mommy says they crack off your teeth."

Collette sighed. "We aren't going to eat your valentine box. Besides, this doesn't have to be a work of art, Laura. Let's just glue a few more hearts on it and it will be fine."

Laura nodded. "Just make it pretty."

Stevie's toy car sped into the kitchen and he crawled behind it. "Here comes the snowplow."

"Watch out, Stevie," said Collette as she pulled open the drawer and got out the large black scissors.

"Hey, can I cut something?" asked Stevie.

"No," Laura said quickly. "We only have two sheets of red paper left and you can't mess them up, right, Collette?"

"Right," said Collette. "Stevie, this is very important, so just go play. Okay, Laura. Where is the paper?"

Laura's eyes flew open. "You had it."

"I didn't have it. I came in to start the cookies and I told you to get the valentine stuff ready."

Laura frowned and blinked. "I did. I put it all right on the couch."

"Was it red paper?" asked Stevie slowly. "Like *all* red?"

Laura nodded. "Two big, big sheets, Stevie. Did you see them?"

Collette could tell by the worried expression on Stevie's face that he had seen them all right.

"But the red paper I saw was *old* paper," insisted Stevie. "It was so old I threw it in the fire."

"What?" cried Collette. She ran past Stevie and hurried into the living room. The logs in the fire were smaller now, streaked with white. There was no red paper in sight, only dark ashes.

"Now what am I going to do?" wailed Laura.

"That's it. I'm not going to school at all anymore. I quit the second grade."

Marsha laughed. "Sister Mary Elizabeth will find you and come after you."

Laura flung herself on the couch. "Well, I'm not going to school without my valentine box."

Collette slumped into a chair, leaning her head against her hand. Maybe things were always this hectic and crazy and she had just never noticed it before, because she had been part of it. Trying to solve the craziness made it stand out a lot more.

"Laura, I know how to make your box look pretty." Stevie took a careful step toward Laura.

Laura covered her ears. "Don't talk to me, Stevie Murphy, because I am very mad at you."

Stevie turned. His face was all scrunched up like he was going to start crying any minute. "Wait seven or one minute. I know what we can do."

"I'm listening, Stevie," said Collette. She was ready for anyone with a plan since she was fresh out of them.

Stevie put his hand into Collette's and started to smile. "We'll just go outside on our street. *Lots* of people have big fancy hearts taped right to their windows. We can ask to borrow one."

Jeff shook his head. "You are *so* dumb, Stevie. You can't ask to *borrow* someone's heart. It's not like borrowing a cup of sugar."

The room was quiet as everyone thought about it. Laura sat up straighter and brushed back her hair. "Yeah, but this time maybe Stevie isn't being real dumb, Jeff. 'Cause I think Mrs. Nassar has three hearts. Her kids are all big now. She wouldn't mind if we borrowed one."

Collette was glad Laura was willing to give it a try. Her father was going to be home any minute and she wanted everyone to be in a good mood when he walked in the door.

"It's worth a try. Let me call her and see if we can have one," said Collette. She dialed the number, then frowned. Busy!

"Let's just walk over," suggested Laura. "We can't get lost since it's right outside."

"Yeah," added Stevie.

Collette dialed the number two more times and then nodded her head. "Well, okay. But you guys have to bundle up," reminded Collette. "And don't stay out too long. It's freezing."

124

"And don't lick anyone's doorknob," added Marsha. She helped bundle Laura, and Collette wrapped two scarves around Stevie's face.

"Be back in five minutes," said Jeff, checking the clock. "Or else you'll be frozen stiff and we'll have to use the hair dryer to thaw you out."

Collette, Marsha, and Jeff watched from the window as Stevie and Laura ran down the driveway and turned up the sidewalk. Mrs. Nassar lived two doors up and would be happy to sweep them inside to warm up and offer them a red heart. Collette waved from the window. As she turned, she smelled something terrible! Something was burning! The dying fire looked fine. It wasn't until Collette glanced to the left and into the kitchen that she saw the thick gray smoke rising lazily to the ceiling. She ran down the hall, yanked open the oven door, and a gush of thick gray smoke burst out. Grabbing a towel for her nose and a pot holder to grip the pizza tray, Collette pulled the cookies out and tossed them into the empty sink.

"Holy cow, what's going on?" cried Marsha. "Get some air in here."

"I know, I know," cried Collette. She dropped

the pot holder and towel and waved the smoke from her eyes.

Collette was so busy unlocking the kitchen window and coughing, she barely jumped when the smoke alarm went off.

Chapter Sixteen

"At least the smoke alarm finally turned off," said Collette.

"There's no way I'm taking in those burned-up lumps," insisted Jeff. He took one from the pizza tin and sailed it out through the open window.

Collette didn't even bother to offer to try and fix the cookies up with frosting and a cherry. They were definitely unfixable. In fact, Jeff's cookies were so burned and shriveled, they should be used as cinders out on the snowy roads.

"I'm really sorry, Jeff," said Collette. "I guess we weren't listening for the buzzer."

Marsha pulled on her hair. "It's my fault. I forgot to turn the timer on. I'm sorry."

"Oh, brother. I thought you two knew what you were doing." Jeff sat down hard in a chair. "Now what am I supposed to do? Sister Elaine gets so mad when you forget to bring things in. I'll probably have to go pick gum off the pews in church."

Collette and Marsha laughed. The nuns at Sacred Heart were always threatening the children with awful punishments like that, but they never followed through.

They cleaned up the messy kitchen. Marsha wrapped up the cookies in foil while Collette closed the window.

"My mom should be here any minute," said Marsha. "At least most of the smoke is out."

"Hey!" Collette turned around and grinned. "Your mom said she was going to bring home lots of those little cakes from the luncheon, right?"

Marsha nodded. "Yeah, she must have had ten dozen in the back of our car this morning."

Collette smiled at her brother. "You can take in a plate of them. You'll have the best treat at the party, Jeff."

"As soon as I get the cookies I'm going to hide them so Stevie can't destroy them before morning."

128

Collette bent down and looked out the window. "Hey — where *is* Stevie anyway? It shouldn't have taken them this long to borrow a heart from Mrs. Nassar."

Marsha gasped. "Oh, no . . . I just remembered that Mrs. Nassar went with my mom this morning to help with the old ladies. I hope they didn't go outside for nothing. It's really cold out there."

"They probably went down to the Cillos'. Mrs. Cillo is always home," said Jeff. "Except they probably won't get a heart there, 'cause Mrs. Cillo's little kids would cry if Stevie tried to take their decorations."

Collette walked down the hall and peeked out the living room windows. "It's already getting dark. I can't see them anywhere."

Marsha laughed. "Collette, relax. We live on a dead end street. How could anyone get lost?"

Jeff nodded. "Yeah. They would have to get kidnapped to disappear."

"Jeff!" Collette's heart started to beat faster and faster. "Don't even joke about something like that." Why weren't they back yet? It was much too cold outside for Stevie and Laura to stop and play. They could have gone to ten houses by now and still have been home twenty minutes ago.

"I'm going to go look for them." Collette kicked off her tennis shoes and picked up her boots. "Jeff, stay here in case Mom needs anything. And don't tell her we lost the little guys."

Jeff made a face. "I won't. I'm not *that* dumb, Collette."

Marsha picked up her boots. "I'll come with you, Collette. Do you think we should take a snapshot of Laura and Stevie?"

Collette's heart nearly flew out of her mouth. "Marsha, we will not be talking to the police or anything. Everyone on the street knows what they look like. I bet we see both of them running up the sidewalk the moment we go outside."

Marsha let out a long breath. "Yeah, well I hope so. Your mom wouldn't stay in bed long if she knew you'd lost them."

"I didn't *lose* them, Marsha." Collette tried not to shout.

Marsha jammed her ski hat down over her ears and yanked the door open. "Jeff, if my mom calls, tell her I'll be right back."

Collette swung her scarf around her neck. "If

Mom asks, just . . . just tell her we went outside for some fresh air."

Jeff looked worried. "But when Dad gets home I'm telling *him* the truth. He'll know what to do."

Collette's back went poker stiff. "*I* know what to do, too, Jeff. Going out to look for them is what any grown-up sitter would do."

Jeff stared at Collette, then shrugged. "Yeah, but you have to admit, Collette . . . those grown-up sitters never lose kids."

Collette turned and followed Marsha outside. She bent her head down against the wind and followed the kelly green and hot pink of Marsha's jacket.

Over half the houses on Browning Street were still dark, creating two long rows of spooky shadows and dark nooks. Collette shivered and pulled up her scarf. She couldn't see or hear the little guys. It was so quiet on the street, you could hear Mrs. Nassar's dog barking from an upstairs window.

"See anything, Marsha?" Collette tried to hurry along on the icy sidewalk. The ice was thick and uneven. Maybe Laura and Stevie had both fallen and slid down the manhole. Collette shook her head to get rid of such awful images. Laura and Stevie were probably both sitting in Mrs. Cillo's bright kitchen, eating cookies and having a great time.

Marsha and Collette both called, "Stevie, Laura," a dozen times as they made their way down to the end of the street. No lights on at the Nassars', Cillos' or Kings'. Total blackness at the dark redbrick house with the black wrought-iron fence at the dead end.

Marsha slowed down and waited for Collette. "I don't know where they could be. The only house left with a light on is . . ." Marsha shivered. "The cat lady's! Stevie and Laura would *never* go there."

Collette's eyes darted toward the tall pine trees nearly blocking the narrow three-story house at the very end of the street. The cat lady's house! No kids except total strangers ever knocked on her door at Halloween. No one ever saw anyone come in or out except the elderly maid who pulled up in a cab every morning at seven-fifteen.

"Stevie and Laura are both scared of her be-cause of all the spooky stories," whispered Collette. "Stevie is even afraid of that house in the daylight."

Marsha shrugged. "Laura may have talked him into it. She really wants those hearts."

Collette shook her head. Nothing could convince Laura and Stevie to walk past the overgrown hedge and knock on the huge double doors.

"They're inside," whispered Marsha. "I know it."

"You're nuts, Marsha. No way!"

Marsha pointed toward the house, her mitten directed to the dimly lit upstairs window. Collette watched as Marsha's confident smile disappeared and her eyes filled with fear. Collette turned and followed Marsha's mitten. There in the center of the cat lady's upstairs window was a heart. A large red heart with a thick black arrow shot straight through it. And next to the large red heart was a head. It was small and round with lots of curly hair. Stevie!

Chapter Seventeen

"Marsha, that's Stevie's head!" Collette's knees started to shake. Right now she would have given anything to be a full-time kid again. Then she could run back home and drag the baby-sitter out to save Stevie and Laura.

Marsha covered her face with her mittens. "Oh sick, I can't look. You don't think the cat lady ripped off Stevie's head and stuck it in her window like some sort of jack-o'-lantern, do you?"

Collette swatted Marsha on her arm. "Oh, be quiet. Of course not. Now come on and let's go knock on the door and bring Stevie and Laura home before my dad gets back." Collette squinted against the swirling snowflakes as she peered

134

down the dark street. Her father's car was going to be coming around the bend any minute. When it did, Collette wanted to be upstairs with all the little kids. She wanted her father to hug her and be proud, to say she was the best baby-sitter in the world. "Come on, Marsha."

Marsha took a step backwards. "Hey, wait a minute! *You* go up to the door and I'll wait here in case the cat lady pulls you inside. Then *I* can go for help."

"Marsha, those rumors about her eating cats are just a lot of nothing. Come on now. I'm freezing. You said you wanted to help."

Marsha gripped Collette's sleeve. "I do, and I *did*, Collette, *all day*. Did I complain about unsticking Stevie's tongue from my front door, or helping Laura get out of the bathroom? No! And I didn't even mind breathing in all that black kitchen smoke from Jeff's crummy cookies. But there's *no way* I'm going inside the cat lady's house." Marsha's eyes narrowed. "We may never come out."

Collette shook herself free and marched up the walk. If Stevie and Laura had gone inside the cat lady's house, then Collette *had* to go and get them back. Not only was she a paid baby-sitter, she was their big sister.

"Think about it, Collette." Marsha pulled hard on Collette's scarf. "Why don't we just call the police or . . . or the animal rescue squad?"

"Because I'm the *baby-sitter*, that's why. Just go home if you're scared, Marsha. I have to get Stevie and Laura before my dad gets home." Collette marched up the wide front steps and pushed hard against the thick black doorbell. The front door opened almost immediately and Laura rushed out onto the porch.

"Oh, Collette, hi!"

"Where's Stevie?" hissed Marsha from the hedges.

Collette hugged her little sister and looked into the huge hall for Stevie. "Are you okay?"

Laura just laughed and pulled Collette inside. "Sure, Stevie and me have had so much fun. Mrs. White is funny."

"Funny?" asked Marsha. "Is she funny, ha-ha, or funny as in eating stray cats and small children? Is Stevie okay?" Marsha had moved closer to the porch, but she still *looked* terrified.

"Yes, he's in the kitchen with Mrs. White. He

ate too many cookies. Now he says he's going to throw up. You came just in time. Mrs. White says she's too old to carry big strong guys like Stevie."

Marsha poked Collette in the back. "I wonder what she made her cookies out of . . . cat eyes, I bet."

Collette didn't want to believe Marsha, but her heart skipped a beat. The sooner she got Stevie and Laura home, the better.

Stevie came walking out, dragging his coat and holding his stomach. "I ate too much. I think I hear my stomach ripping open."

The elderly lady following Stevie carried a handful of red paper hearts. "Hello, girls. I'm Mrs. White. I told the children they should call home so you wouldn't worry. I guess we lost track of time."

Collette nodded. She had just lost track of hours of her life, baby-sitting. She was exhausted. It wouldn't surprise her to wake up in the morning with ten gray hairs sprouting out of her head. "I'm Collette, their older sister." She handed Laura her coat. "I was really worried, Laura. You should have called."

Marsha took another step closer. "And I'm Marsha Cessano. We live in that real big fancy house on the corner. My mother is due home *any minute* to get me and she'll be real worried if I'm not there." Marsha drew in a deep breath. "My mom calls the police at the drop of a hat."

Both eyebrows shot up on the elderly lady. "Well, I guess you'd all better get going."

Mrs. White took four mittens from the top of her radiator. "Now, children, don't be strangers."

"We won't. Thanks for all the hearts!" laughed Laura.

As soon as they were back on the icy sidewalk, Collette grabbed Stevie's and Laura's hands. "Now you two stay right by my side till Daddy gets home. I can't believe you went in the cat — I mean Mrs. White's house without telling me. I'm the baby-sitter, you know. You're supposed to tell me *everything*!"

"I'm sorry I forgot to call," said Laura. "But Mrs. White kept showing me all her hearts. She used to be an art teacher before she was an old lady."

"Well, this *whole day* is turning *me* into an old lady. How does Mom do this every day?"

Stevie stopped. "Are you really turning into an old lady?"

138

Marsha hooted. "Add a can of powder to her hair tonight, Stevie."

Collette kept walking, pulling Stevie along. "No, but you kids are a lot of work."

Laura stopped. "Are we . . . are we *too much work*, Collette?"

Collette turned, seeing the sadness beginning to cloud over Laura's face. "Well, no."

"It that why Mommy's sick in bed? Did we wear her all the way out?"

Stevie grabbed onto Collette's arm. "Is Mommy an old lady, too?"

Collette and Marsha both grinned at each other. "No, and Mom isn't worn out. She's . . . she's pregnant. That's all. She's feeling a lot better now, too."

Laura and Stevie both nodded.

"Once, when my friend Joey's dog got pregnant, he chewed up a whole newspaper and threw up," confided Stevie.

"And my friend's cat eats grass when she's pregnant," added Laura.

Collette started walking faster. Marsha caught up and took Laura's hand. "So, you want a new sister or a brother, Laura?"

Laura frowned. "I'm not allowed to get rid of Stevie, Mommy said."

"Yeah," agreed Stevie. "I get to stay here forever."

Collette sighed. "No, Marsha means the new baby."

Laura shrugged, then grinned. "I guess maybe I want one of *each* so we will have four boys and four girls." She smiled up at Collette. "Is that what you want, too?"

Collette nodded quickly, a little too tired right now to even *think* about being responsible for one more brother or sister. Being the oldest used to be hard because her brothers and Laura got in the way all the time. Now that she was older and smarter she realized that *that* was nothing. Being the oldest now was *really* hard because you had to watch out for them all, help them with their projects and problems, and make sure they didn't hurt themselves by doing dumb stuff that only a little kid would think to do.

Collette sighed again as she turned into the driveway. She must be doing something wrong. Sure, her mother got tired some days, but she never acted like Collette felt. Every bone in Collette's body ached and her head felt like a soggy orange into which somebody had spent the whole day pounding a bag full of nails.

Collette dropped Stevie's hand to yank open the side door. "And don't track in any more snow," she snapped. "I'm tired of cleaning up puddles." Collette heard how mean she sounded. Even Marsha looked startled before carefully kicking both boots against the milk box.

"Well, it's *about time*!" cried Jeff. "Where were you guys, anyway? I was just about to wake up Mom. And Dad called to say he was on the way home and I had to lie and say you couldn't come to the phone 'cause you were helping Laura with her valentine box." Jeff scowled. "Boy, if you're a good baby-sitter, you're supposed to be in the house and know where all the kids are at all times, Collette."

For a second, Collette thought she was going to either faint or explode. "Well, I guess I won't win the baby-sitter-of-the-week award then, will I, Jeff?"

Marsha started to laugh.

"It isn't funny, Marsha!" Collette's voice was almost a whisper now, as if her plug had been pulled.

Collette slumped down on the bottom step. "I give up. I surrender. In fact, I quit."

Jeff looked worried. He took a step closer to the stairs. "Hey, I was only kidding. I just wondered where you guys were 'cause it was so dark and . . ."

Collette's nose tingled. Soon her eyes would start burning and then she would just start bawling the way she did when she was little and her parents left her with a strange new baby-sitter. Why did she ever think she could replace her mother, even for twelve hours?

Marsha rammed her feet back in her boots and put her hand on the door. "Well, this has been fun, but I guess I'd better go back over and see if my mom is home yet."

Stevie kept his eyes on Collette, but took a step closer to Marsha like he might just want to go home with her.

"I'll send the leftover cakes and cookies, Jeff," offered Marsha.

Jeff nodded. Then, glancing at Collette, he

shrugged. "Except, if your mom ate them all, that's okay, too. The cookies Collette made will be sort of okay."

Laura nodded. "Yeah. Just don't tell the kids that they were supposed to be cookies, right, Collette."

Marsha grinned and pulled open the door. "Well, let me know if you need them. I'll call you later, Collette."

As soon as Marsha left, Collette leaned her head against the wall and decided she should stay on the stairs until her dad came home to take over. That way she was sure not to burn another cookie, lose another kid, or feel another bit sorrier for herself. Collette sighed. She had been a flop as a baby-sitter. She had gone from *perfect* with her father over breakfast, to *mad* at all three kids before dinner.

"Are you real mad at us?" asked Laura.

Collette stood up, taking in a deep breath. "No. I'm not mad. I guess I'm just tired, Laura. I have been acting like a baby-sitter all day and now I'm worn out. I'm just a kid, okay? So why don't you guys just go downstairs and watch television or something? Do anything except ask me to do something. I want to just . . . just sit down and not do a thing, okay? Daddy will be home soon."

Stevie nodded. "Don't tell Daddy we were bad."

Collette gave a small smile. "Yeah, well, I'll make you a deal. *I* won't say a word about you guys, and *you* promise not to tell Daddy I wasn't a good baby-sitter."

Laura, Jeff, and Stevie all looked shocked. Jeff reached out and grabbed Collette's elbow. "Hey, you *were* good, Collette. You were better than lots of *real* baby-sitters."

Laura nodded. "Yeah, I think Daddy should pay you lots of money."

"Daddy should give you ten hundred and twenty-eleven dollars, Collette. You didn't make me take one nap, not even when I dumped white powder on Mommy's head or got sticked to Marsha's door." Stevie grinned. "You were gooder than Debbie."

Collette smiled back at her brothers and sister. It was nice to hear them cast their vote for her. Maybe she hadn't done such a terrible job after all. "Thanks. I don't know how Mom does this kind of stuff and . . ."

"What's that?" Jeff turned. "Who's coughing? Is that Mom?"

Collette almost knocked Stevie over as she raced up the stairs to the landing. "Mom, are you okay?" If her mother was throwing up again, it would be a *real* bad sign.

From the landing, Collette saw her mother sitting on the top step. Her face was in her hands and her shoulders were shaking. Tiny flakes of baby powder were drifting down from her head.

"Mom!" cried Collette, rushing up the rest of the stairs. "Oh, my gosh, are you okay? You should have stayed in bed."

Mrs. Murphy looked up, laughing so hard she had tears in her eyes. Collette stood frozen, staring at her mother.

"Oh, honey, I didn't mean to scare you, but . . ." Mrs. Murphy started laughing again. "You kids are so funny."

Collette sat beside her mother and started to smile. Boy, was it great to see her mom this happy. Nothing could be wrong with the baby if her mother was laughing so hard.

"Is Mom okay?" called Jeff from the bottom of the stairs.

"Yeah, she's just laughing," called back Collette. She turned to her mother and grinned. "But why are you laughing? What's so funny?"

"You," Mrs. Murphy said softly. "I got out of bed to see if Daddy was home yet and I heard you talking to the children."

Collette's smile disappeared. "Well, yeah, I guess I was just tired and . . . I know baby-sitters aren't supposed to act that way, but . . ."

Mrs. Murphy shook her head. "I was laughing because . . . because you sounded just like me."

"I did?" Collette thought for a second. Her mother never said she was going to quit. Her mother always acted happy to be a mom.

"Well, not the same words, but . . ." Mrs. Murphy put her arm around Collette. "You needed to remind the children that you're not a robot. Everyone gets tired. I think it's very grown-up to admit when you need some peace and quiet. And it's good for the other children to realize that, too."

Collette smiled. Boy, it was great the way her mother put it. Her mother made it seem like losing her temper had been the perfect thing to do.

"Daddy's home!" cried Stevie. He pounded up

the stairs and flung his arms around his mother. "He has pizza!"

Collette could feel the gust of cold air as the side door opened. She listened to the laughter below, the happy voices talking about the fire they had built that afternoon, and the great red valentines Laura was pasting on her box for school tomorrow. Collette held her breath and waited for someone to mention the locked bathroom door, the smoke alarm, or Collette announcing she was going to quit. But there was only more laughter and the smell of hot pepperoni pizza drifting up the stairway.

"You'd better go down and get your paycheck and some pizza," laughed her mother. She kissed Collette on the cheek. "Thank you *again* for being such a help, today. I feel so much better. I actually slept."

Collette's eyes widened. "You did?"

Mrs. Murphy nodded. "Yes, I was just so relaxed with you being in charge." She reached out and tapped Collette on the nose. "I'm lucky I have you right under my roof. Good help is so hard to find."

Collette stood up and smiled back. "I'll help a lot with the new baby, too." She put her hand on the banister, then turned back. "Mom. Things are going to be okay with the baby, aren't they?" Collette held her breath.

Finally, her mother nodded. "I think I'm going to be all right. Pretty soon you will have *another* Murphy to baby-sit. Think you can handle that?"

"Yes," laughed Collette. "I mean, I may crack up a few times and think I won't be able to do everything you need me to help out with. But that's normal stuff."

"Normal stuff." Mrs. Murphy laughed. "Now run downstairs and get some dinner and relax."

Collette bent down and kissed her mother's cheek. "First I'll bring you up some pizza and a big glass of milk." Collette galloped down the steps, two at a time. As she raced into the kitchen she started to laugh. Boy did it feel good to be off duty. And since she was officially off the payroll, she gave her father a big hug. Taking care of everyone all day had been a busy job. Kind of a dress rehearsal for being a mother. Collette gave her father another tight squeeze and leaned her head against his chest. She was glad to have him home at last, glad he was in charge now. Collette closed her eyes. She was so tired. Being a pretend little Mother Murphy had been a busy, full-time job. One day had seemed like forever.

"Hey, Daddy, look at my valentine box," cried Laura. She ran into the room and plopped her freshly glued box down on the kitchen table. "It finally looks like a real good valentine box. Mrs. White is the nice old lady who lives down the street. She told Stevie and me that she would never eat a cat and she gave me three hearts and she showed me how to make two special valentine hearts all by myself." Laura drew in a deep breath and held up two large red hearts. "One is for Mommy since she is the best mommy in the whole world, and one is for Collette." Laura grinned. "You're not a real mommy, but you're the bestest sister in the *whole* world."

"At least in Pittsburgh," Jeff added. His face blushed red as everyone laughed.

Collette walked over to Laura and took the large paper heart in her hand. "Thanks, guys."

Stevie ran up and tackled Collette hard around

the waist. "Yeah, Collette. We like you so don't think you can ever run away from us, 'cause you can't."

Collette felt her father's warm hand on her neck. Right now she was so tired she couldn't think of running *anywhere*.

"Well, I'd better go upstairs and say hello to your mother," said Mr. Murphy. "But first, let me pay the baby-sitter."

"And the kids!" laughed Jeff. "We told her what to do."

Collette grinned. She watched her father reach into his back pocket and pull out his shiny black leather wallet. He handed Collette the money and smiled. "Thanks for helping out, Collette."

"Boy, are you rich!" cried Stevie.

"Thanks, Dad. I can help out tomorrow, too." Collette said. "For free."

Mr. Murphy smiled. "Thanks, honey, but instead of having a sitter, your grandmother will be here tomorrow. She called right before I left the office."

Collette smiled. She knew her mother would enjoy being treated like a kid again by her own mother.

"Your mother sounded so rested and relaxed on the phone that I decided to give you a *tip*, Collette," added Mr. Murphy.

"More money!" cried Jeff. "Holy cow!"

Collette looked up at her father. "No, that's okay. You gave me too much already!" If her dad tried to give her *more money* she might have to tell him about some of her mistakes.

Mr. Murphy reached into his back pocket again. He pulled out his hand and held a small package out to Collette. "Your mother and I really want you to have this."

"Dad, really, I . . ."

"Take it, Collette," laughed Jeff. "Then you can give it to me."

"I think you might need it on Saturday." Mr. Murphy dropped the small roll into her hand.

Stevie pushed forward. "Open it, Collette. Maybe it's candy."

Collette started to tug at the tape wrapped around the brown paper. "It's so tiny." Finally she unrolled a thin tube of Chap Stick onto the palm of her hand.

Chap Stick?

"Ohhhh, you lucky," said Laura. "You got lipstick."

Mr. Murphy reached out and hugged Collette. "It's special lipstick . . . for skiers. It gets pretty cold up at Seven Springs."

"Seven Springs? You mean . . . I can go on the ski trip . . . with Marsha and Sarah?" Collette was laughing so hard she could hardly get the words out.

"And take me, too, Collette!" begged Stevie. "And Laura."

"Can I go, Dad?" asked Jeff.

Mr. Murphy shook his head. "When you're older. Your mother and I thought Collette might enjoy the day off."

"Thanks, Dad!" A rush of icy prickles raced up Collette's arms. The kitchen windows rattled with another gust of wintery wind and the temperature was dropping by the hour. But Collette knew her goose bumps weren't caused from the cold. They were all coming from deep inside. Collette shivered and then slowly pulled her sweater sleeves down over each arm. She didn't want these goose bumps to fade away too fast. They felt too good; she had earned every one!